GOODLY AND GRAVE

In a Case of Bad Magic

JUSTINE WINDSOR

ILLUSTRATED BY BECKA MOOR

HarperCollins *Children's Books*

First published in Great Britain by
HarperCollins *Children's Books* in 2018
HarperCollins *Children's Books* is a division of HarperCollins*Publishers* Ltd,
HarperCollins Publishers
1 London Bridge Street
London SE1 9GF

The HarperCollins website address is:
www.harpercollins.co.uk
1

ISBN 978–0–00–818359–2

Justine Windsor and Becka Moor assert the moral right to be identified as
the author and illustrator of the work respectively.

Typeset in Lido STF 12/18pt by Palimpsest Book Production Limited
Falkirk, Stirlingshire
Printed and bound in England by CPI Group (UK) Ltd, Croydon CR0 4YY

MIX
Paper from
responsible sources
FSC www.fsc.org **FSC® C007454**

This book is produced from independently certified FSC™ paper
to ensure responsible forest management.

For more information visit: www.harpercollins.co.uk/green

For Chas 'n' Pheebs

CHAPTER ONE

A BALL OF MAGIC

Lucy Goodly dodged sideways. A flurry of sparks whizzed past, just missing her ear. Instead they hit the chimney breast behind her and sputtered out, leaving a faint smell of burning as well as a large scorch mark on Lady Tabitha Grave's nose. Not the real Lady Tabitha Grave, but her portrait, which hung over the fireplace.

"Excellent!" said Lord Grave. "Your turn now. Concentrate. Create your own attack sparks and return fire!" Bathsheba, Lord Grave's black panther,

blinked her yellow eyes before slinking off behind one of the sofas, as though she understood what was about to happen.

Lucy narrowed her eyes and focused her thoughts on the spell in hand. As Lord Grave had instructed her earlier, she imagined all the warmth in her body rushing towards her fingers. As she did so, her fingertips grew hotter and hotter until they felt as though they would burst into flames. When she felt she couldn't bear the heat a second longer, she raised her hand behind her head, and then, as if she was throwing an invisible ball, flung it forward. The orange-red sparks that were clustered around her fingers flew off like tiny flies and hurtled towards Lord Grave, who ducked. But he was a smidgeon too late and the sparks grazed the crown of his top hat. Lord Grave whipped it off and beat the sparks out before they could do too much damage. Lucy folded her arms and smiled in satisfaction.

"Impressive!" Lord Grave said. "Now, as I have just demonstrated, you might not always be able to get out of the path of an attack spark. And a magician

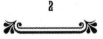

skilled in this particular art might be able to create a spark that will track you if you try to flee from it. However, there is a technique that—"

There was a knock at the drawing-room door.

"Who is it?" Lord Grave called.

"It's Violet, sir."

"One moment!" Lord Grave put his hat back on. Then he hurried over to the window and opened it in order to dispel the smell of burning before calling Violet in.

"Please, sir. Mrs Crawley wants to know if you can spare Lucy for a while. She needs us to fetch some ingredients for the ball," Violet said shyly. She was a small mousey-haired girl three or four years younger than Lucy, who was twelve. Caruthers, Violet's knitted frog which she carried everywhere with her, was tucked into her apron pocket.

"Very well. Lucy has finished her . . . dusting, I think, so she's free to go."

"Thank you, sir. Oh my, look at Lady Grave! Her nose has gone all black!"

"What? Oh yes. Don't worry, Violet, it's soot from

the fire, I expect. Becky can deal with it later. Now, off you go," Lord Grave said. Of course he couldn't tell Violet the real reason for Lady Grave's blackened nose. The little scullery maid had no idea that her employer was a magician – as were most of the other staff at Grave Hall.

"Thank you, sir." Violet gave Lord Grave a timid curtsey and then the two girls left the drawing room and headed for the kitchen.

"He's up to no good!" Violet said as they hurried downstairs.

"What do you mean?" Lucy replied cautiously.

"I could smell smoke. He's been puffing on his cigars in secret, hasn't he? Master Bertie will be very cross if he finds out!"

Master Bertie was Lord Grave's son. Surprisingly, Bertie hadn't inherited his father's magical ability. In fact, Bertie didn't even believe in magic, arguing that it could all be explained by science.

Lucy breathed a quiet sigh of relief. She'd worried for a moment that Violet might have seen traces of the attack sparks in the drawing room and become

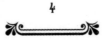

suspicious. Although most non-magical grown-ups wouldn't have noticed magic if it bit them on the ear, non-magical children were a different matter. Their minds were still developing and much more open, so it wasn't unknown for them to be able to see spells being cast. Because of this, all the magicians who lived at or visited Grave Hall were careful how they used their talents whenever Violet, and Becky, the under-housemaid, were around.

✳

Down in the kitchen, Mrs Crawley, Grave Hall's cook-cum-housekeeper, was in a high state of anxiety. Potatoes, carrots, bags of flour and sugar, and a large bunch of stinging nettles were strewn across the huge kitchen table. Mrs Crawley was bent over the cooking range, which crouched in the chimney breast. Today her long beard was fastened in a bun on her chin. It looked like a giant, hairy spot. The reason for this unusual beard style was to stop it trailing in the numerous pots and pans that were bubbling away.

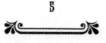

A ginger cat was lying in front of the kitchen range, warming itself. It was not the most attractive of cats with its one and a half ears, missing eye and truncated tail.

"Look at Smell. He's so lazy!" Violet exclaimed, before going over to tickle the cat under the chin. Smell was named for his unfortunate propensity for producing whiffs that could knock a person out if they got too close. Being a magical cat, he also had the ability to speak, but of course he never did so in front of Violet and Becky, or anyone else non-magical.

The heat in the kitchen was stifling and for once Lucy wished she was wearing a frock instead of her customary breeches, shirt and jacket. Mrs Crawley always said that frocks kept the nether regions cool in a hot kitchen and that was why she preferred to wear them herself, even though she was actually a man. Lucy had been very confused by this when she first met Mrs Crawley but, as Mrs Crawley had pointed out, it wasn't usual for girls to wear breeches, so she and Lucy had something in common in their unconventional clothing choices. Mrs Crawley's name was also something Lucy had found puzzling at first. But now she was familiar with Lord Grave's insistence on sticking with certain traditions, one of them being that the cook should always be known as "Mrs" regardless of marital status or gender.

Vonk, the butler, who was small man, as short as Lucy in fact, was sitting at the kitchen table. His shirtsleeves were rolled up and he was carefully polishing the best silver cutlery. At the same time, he and Mrs Crawley seemed to be having words.

"Mrs C, I really don't think that's wise," Vonk was saying, pointing the tines of the fork he was cleaning at the bunch of nettles that lay on the table. "Lord Grave said no experimental dishes for the feast."

"Vonk, nettle pudding is hardly experimental. I found the recipe in an ancient cookbook. Many magicians ate it in olden times."

"Wouldn't nettle pudding sting your mouth?" Lucy asked.

"A good point!" Vonk replied.

Mrs Crawley chuckled. "Of course it won't.

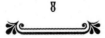

Cooking takes the sting out of them! I'm sure you girls will like it when you try it!"

Lucy and Violet exchanged disgusted looks. Mrs Crawley was a little too avant-garde at times with her cooking. Only that morning she had tried to tempt them both with bacon and frogspawn for breakfast.

✳

Once they'd obtained the shopping list from Mrs Crawley, Lucy and Violet left their fellow servants to carry on bickering about menus, and set off towards Grave Village. The trees that lined the rough road leading to the village were beginning to look rather bare, their branches dark and spiky against the grey October sky. Lucy and Violet scrunched their way through the piles of red, yellow and purple leaves strewn underfoot. A fine rain began to fall, so they put the hoods of their winter cloaks up. Violet began chattering about the preparations for the ball.

"I wish I was working on the big night. I don't know why Lord Grave is giving me and Becky the

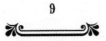

day of the ball off. I hope you'll be all right on your own." Violet looked anxiously at Lucy.

"I'll be fine. Vonk and Mrs Crawley will be here." Lucy knew that Lord Grave had decided Violet and Becky should be absent from Grave Hall on the day of the ball, in case either of them noticed any magical activity. Lucy really didn't mind being the only maid on duty. In fact, she couldn't wait for the ball. Magicians from all over the world were due to attend, and Lord Grave had promised to introduce her to them. According to him, magicians liked to show off and try to out-magic each other at these sorts of events, so the ball promised to be a spectacular affair.

Lord Grave had also told Lucy that the ball was being held to celebrate the one hundredth anniversary of the defeat of a very wicked magician called Hester Coin, by Lord Grave's great-grandmother, Lady Constance Grave. Although Lady Constance had successfully vanquished Hester Coin, she had been worried that other corrupt magicians might undertake similar criminal activities in the future. So she'd created Magicians Against the Abuse of

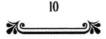

Magic, otherwise known as MAAM, to combat such threats.

Since then, the head of MAAM had always been a member of the Grave family, apart from one recent period of a few years when the current Lord Grave had been too sad and heartsick at the disappearance of his son Bertie to bother with MAAM duties. But Lucy had changed all that when she had rescued Bertie from Amethyst Shade, the wicked magician who had kidnapped him. Now Lucy herself was a proud member of MAAM. Of course Violet didn't know any of this. As far as she knew, the ball was to celebrate Bertie's return home.

Naturally, Lucy had been very keen to find out exactly what Hester Coin had done that was so bad. However, Lord Grave had refused to tell her.

"She committed so many crimes, it would take too long to explain them all. And, for various reasons, we don't like her last and most heinous crime to be widely known. She was finally defeated here at Grave Hall, and only we Graves and Lord Percy's family know the full details."

Although she was warm and toasty inside her thick cloak, Lucy couldn't help shivering a little as she remembered the look on Lord Grave's face when he'd said this. He'd looked afraid. Lord Grave was a courageous man who didn't scare easily, so Hester Coin must have done something very bad indeed.

CHAPTER TWO

THE BOY IN THE ALLEY

After about an hour, Lucy and Violet reached St Isan's, the old church that stood at the edge of Grave Village. The church clock began to chime eleven, sending the crows perched on the spire flapping and cawing into the sky. By now the rain had stopped and the sun had come out, although the day was still chilly. The two girls pushed back the hoods of their cloaks as they took a shortcut through the graveyard to reach the high road where the shops were. Violet murmured to

Caruthers in a soothing manner as they walked.

"Don't worry. It's daytime. All the ghosties will be asleep," she told him.

The two girls picked their way between the gravestones. Some were very old and spotted with lichen, their inscriptions faded. Violet pointed to a particularly decrepit one, which leaned over at an angle.

"Look, Lucy. When a gravestone's all lopsided like that it means the person buried under it's been trying to get out," she said in a hushed voice, her eyes wide.

"Who told you that?" Lucy asked.

"Becky."

Lucy sighed. Becky loved to tease and scare Violet. "That's a load of rubbish! Don't believe anything she says."

They left the graveyard behind, and headed through the church gate out into Grave Village high street. It was a bustling place. People hurried to and fro across the cobbled pavements, and horses and carts rumbled along the road. There were plenty of shops to visit. There was a draper's, where Violet's mother worked as a seamstress; a candle-maker; a butcher's and a greengrocer's. There was also a shop called Busby's Buns that sold confectionary and cakes. Violet immediately dragged Lucy to the window of this shop where all sorts of delicious indulgences were on display. There were buns oozing cream, tarts with glossy jewel-coloured fruit fillings, as well as chocolate-covered gingerbread men – Lucy's favourite. Her mouth watered as she imagined the spicy-sweet taste of them.

"Shall we go in and spend our threepenny bits?" Violet asked. Mrs Crawley had generously given each of them one of the silver coins to buy themselves a treat.

"Let's wait until we've done the shopping," Lucy replied. "Where is it we have to go?"

"Surprising Supplies. The owner is Mrs Crawley's cousin twice removed, isn't she, Caruthers?"

Lucy wondered if Mrs Crawley's cousin twice removed was a magician, but of course she couldn't ask Violet this. "I'm guessing that means it's an unusual sort of shop?"

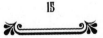

"Ooh, yes. It sells some very odd things, like powdered worms and ants soaked in brandy," Violet said, wrinkling her nose. "We have to go down that alleyway to get to it."

Violet pointed to a narrow alley, which ran between the butcher's shop and The Grave's End, the village pub. There was a tall blonde girl, aged about sixteen, standing near the entrance to the alleyway. She was holding a violin, and a large, shaggy brown-and-white dog sat at her heels, panting. Its breath steamed in the cold air. The girl tucked her violin under her chin and began to play it as Lucy and Violet approached. The tune was a very popular one about a man deceived by his sweetheart. Violet began softly singing some of the words that accompanied it. "*The mask she wore, the mask she wore, to hide herself from me . . .*"

Lucy was about to enter the alleyway when Violet suddenly stopped singing and grabbed her sleeve, pulling her back.

"What's wrong?"

"It's Caruthers. He's scared. It's too dark down there."

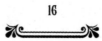

Lucy peered into the alleyway. It *was* rather narrow and gloomy. "What about all the times you've been here before? Caruthers wasn't scared then, was he?"

Violet shook her head. "No, but that's because Mrs Crawley was with us. She's tall and strong. He felt safe with her."

"We can hold hands if you're scared, Violet."

"*I'm* not scared," Violet insisted. "It's Caruthers. He doesn't think I'm big enough to defend him from robbers."

Lucy sighed. "What about if I look after Caruthers?"

"That's a good idea. And we could hold hands, I suppose, to make him feel extra safe."

Violet handed Caruthers to Lucy, who stuck the little knitted frog down the front of her cloak, so that only his button-eyed head peeped out. Then she took Violet's hand and the two of them stepped into the alley. Although Lucy had been rather dismissive of Violet's fears, she felt a prickle of unease as they left the autumn sunshine for the gloomy dankness of the alley. There were no cobbles to walk on and the ground was muddy underfoot. Lucy was glad she was wearing her sturdy winter boots, as there were filthy puddles to splash through.

They were halfway down the alley when they heard a noise.

"Awwww! Awwww!"

"What's that?" Violet said, clutching Lucy's arm.

"I don't know."

"We should go back!"

"Awwww! Awwww!"

"I think someone's hurt," Lucy said. She gathered her courage and ventured a little way further into the alley, with Violet still grasping her sleeve. A very strange sight soon met their eyes. A boy around the same age as Violet was sitting in one of the mucky pools of water, sobbing loudly. He had golden curly hair and a chubby, cherub-like face, which was streaked with dirt, as was his neck. His gaze flickered first towards Lucy, then to Violet.

"Miss, you've a kind face!" he said to her. "Please help me!"

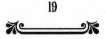

"Oh, of course I will!" Violet said, her fear forgotten. She moved closer to the boy. "Whatever's the matter? Are you hurt?"

"He stole my bun money!" the boy wailed. "I've been saving up for buns for my mum's birthday tea. It's taken me months. And he stole it! Awww! Awww!"

"Who did?" Lucy asked. She had to shout to be heard above the din. Although she felt sorry for the boy, the dreadful wailing was rather wearing on the ears.

"A big brute of a lad! And now there'll be no buns for tea!"

"How horrid!" Violet replied. "But do stop crying. I've got threepence. You can have that to buy some buns."

The boy looked up at her with a shocked expression on his face. It seemed he was unused to kindness. "Really?"

"Of course! Now, you should get up out of that puddle or your bottom will rot! Then you really will have problems!" Violet said. The serious expression

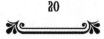

on her face indicated she earnestly believed in bottom-rot.

The boy did as Violet suggested and stood up, muddy water dripping off the seat of his ragged trousers. Violet held out her silver threepenny coin to him.

"You're so kind, miss. I wish I could give you summat in return." He began patting the pockets of his jacket. Lucy frowned as she noticed something puzzling about him. His jacket didn't match his raggedy trousers. It was new-looking and made of good, thick material. Perhaps he'd stolen it? But Lucy didn't have time to dwell on this as by now the boy had found something in his pocket to give Violet. There was a flash of silver as he whipped out a knife.

CHAPTER THREE

WHEN SPARKS ATTACK

The boy leaped at Violet, wielding his blade. He knocked her to the ground, then pinned her down by kneeling on her arms.

Violet shrieked wildly.

Lucy charged towards the boy, her fingers tingling with heat the way they had earlier that morning when she'd been practising magic with Lord Grave. Barely thinking about what she was doing, she drew her hand back and sent a flurry of attack sparks whizzing towards the boy's exposed

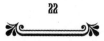

nape, just above his collar. The sparks struck their target perfectly.

The boy screamed in pain, clapping his hand over the back of his neck. Violet managed to free one of her arms and punched the boy. The punch didn't have much power behind it, but it did land somewhere sensitive, and the boy squealed. At the same time, Lucy let fly at him with another volley of sparks. The combined assault completely unbalanced the boy and he ended up flat on his back in the mud. Cursing, he quickly scrambled to his feet, snatching up something he'd dropped. He stepped towards Lucy, clearly considering charging at her. But then he stopped, and for a few seconds he just stared at her, then over his shoulder at Violet, then at Lucy again. His eyes widened.

"*You're* her! I thought she was . . . That *stupid* frog!"

Lucy had expected the boy to demand more money, so his words confused her. Caruthers had fallen out of her cloak during the fight and was now lying with his head in a muddy puddle. What did he have to do with anything?

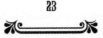

"Leave us alone or I'll hurt you some more!" Lucy yelled. Her heart was pounding so hard she could hardly hear her own voice, which sounded far more threatening than she actually felt. She pointed at the boy, her fingertips stinging with heat again. The boy stepped back, his gaze fixed on the attack sparks that were beginning to crackle around Lucy's hand. Her heart lurched. Not only could the boy feel the sparks, he could *see* them too!

After a moment's hesitation, the boy turned and ran off down the alley. His gait was somewhat lopsided as he splashed through patches of muddy water, no doubt due to Violet's lucky punch.

When the boy was safely out of sight, Lucy hunkered down next to the little scullery maid and helped her sit up. "Violet! Are you all right?"

"He c-cut me!"

"Where?"

Violet held out her right hand. The soft flap of skin between her thumb and forefinger was bleeding.

"Anywhere else?"

Violet shook her head.

"Thank goodness." Lucy took out her handkerchief, which fortunately was freshly washed, and wrapped the wound as best she could. Then she helped Violet to stand up.

"Where's Caruthers?" Violet asked.

"Don't worry, he's here. He's a bit mucky, though." Lucy retrieved Caruthers from the muddy puddle and handed him to Violet, who clutched him to her chest with her uninjured hand. Then the two of them stumbled shakily out of the alley and back on to the high street.

The violin player was the first person to spot they were in trouble. She laid her instrument down in its velvet-lined case and dashed over to them, her shaggy dog trotting alongside her.

"Hell's teeth! What happened to you two?"

"A boy. Attacked her with a knife!" Lucy said.

"He attacked her? What about you? Did he get you?" the girl asked, sounding extremely concerned.

"No, he didn't." Lucy shook her head. She was beginning to feel rather sick at the thought of what might have happened if they hadn't managed to fight

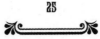

off the boy. By now, some of the shoppers bustling about had noticed something was amiss too. A little crowd began to form round Violet and Lucy.

"Ooh, look at the little one, her hand's bleeding!"

Violet, who had turned very pale, said, "Could someone please fetch my mother?"

"Your mother, chicken?" replied a tall, dark-haired woman.

"She's a seamstress. She works at the draper's." Violet closed her eyes and began swaying dangerously.

"I'll take you to your mother, don't you worry!" The woman quickly scooped Violet up before she could fall and then began heading towards one of the shops at the other end of the street. Lucy hurried after her, stumbling over the cobbles. When the three of them burst into the draper's, the bell hanging above the door jangled madly, startling the man behind the counter. He looked up from the bolt of cloth he was folding and cried out in alarm.

"Brenda! What's going on? Is that little Violet Worthington?" he said.

"Get her mother." Brenda carefully deposited

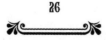

Violet on one of the tall stools that stood in front of the counter. The man swiftly obeyed and hastened through a pair of fringed red curtains that hung behind the counter, concealing the back room of the shop.

"You should sit down too, chicken, you look dreadful," Brenda advised Lucy, who gratefully slumped on to a stool just as Mrs Worthington, a plump woman with kind brown eyes, ran through the curtains. She lifted up a section of the wooden counter and rushed over to Violet.

"My little girl! What's happened to you?" Mrs Worthington took Violet's wounded hand gently in her own and began carefully removing the handkerchief.

"Some lad attacked the two of 'em, down in the alley," Brenda explained.

Mrs Worthington glanced at Lucy. "You must be Lucy, the new boot girl. Violet's always talking about you. Can you tell me what happened, dear?"

As Lucy began explaining the attack once again, Violet laid her head on the shop counter. She was fast asleep by the time Lucy had finished speaking.

"That little one needs to be in bed," Brenda said.

"I'll take her home," Mrs Worthington replied.

"What about you, chicken?" Brenda asked Lucy.

"I'll be fine. I can walk to Grave Hall," Lucy said, although she was so shaken up that she was dreading the long slog back.

"If you like, I can take you. I've got my pony and trap."

Lucy gratefully agreed. She followed Brenda out of the draper's shop to where the pony and trap were standing. Brenda produced an apple from her pocket and gave it to the grey-and-white pony to munch on while she and Lucy climbed up on to the driver's seat.

Lucy fell silent as Brenda geed the horse out of the village and on to the road that led back to Grave Hall. Was she going to be in trouble for casting magic in a public place? And what about the boy? She was certain that he'd seen the attack sparks. What if he started telling everyone what he'd witnessed? Lord Grave would be furious!

"You mustn't worry, Lucy," Brenda said at that

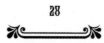

very moment, as though she guessed exactly what Lucy was thinking. "Lord Grave will understand that you had to use magic to defend yourself, I'm sure."

Lucy turned and gaped at her. "You're a . . ."

"That's right. My talents are mostly lowly, but I'm a magician just the same."

"But how did you know I used magic?"

"There were a few little sparks floating around you when you came out of the alley. Now, tell me, how is everyone up at the Hall? Does Mrs Crawley still concoct revolting recipes? Bernie and I were very close when I worked there. I do miss her."

"You used to work at Grave Hall?"

"I was the gardener there."

"Why did you leave?" Lucy asked.

Brenda kept her eyes on the road. "An agricultural difference of opinion, chicken. Lord Grave sacked me. I don't really like to talk about it, to be honest."

✳

Brenda dropped Lucy at the bottom of the long drive which led to Grave Hall.

"Hope you don't mind me leaving you here," she said, gazing rather wistfully towards the house as Lucy clambered to the ground. "Much as I'd like to see Bernie again, I don't want to risk bumping into his Lordship. You take care now."

Lucy waved Brenda off, then began to toil towards the house. When she finally stumbled in to the kitchen, exhausted and relieved, Becky was there, shelling broad beans. Mrs Crawley was too busy attending to some bubbling pots on the range to notice Lucy arrive at first.

Becky gave Lucy an appraising glance. "You took your time, Goodly. You look a right state. Did you have some sort of accident?" Becky's tone of voice suggested she keenly hoped something bad had happened to Lucy,

"Not an accident. Sorry to disappoint you, Becky," Lucy snapped. "I was attacked. So was Violet. She got the worst of it. She got cut by a knife."

"*Violet* got cut?" Becky said, accidently knocking the bowl of beans off the table and on to the floor.

Mrs Crawley turned from the range. Her face was bright red and sweaty from the heat of the pans. She hurried over to Lucy and put an arm round her shoulders, her forehead dripping gently on to Lucy's cloak. She steered her in to one of the kitchen chairs. Lucy was grateful as she was beginning to feel rather odd.

"Vonk! Get in here!" Mrs Crawley cried. "Lucy, are you all right? Where's Violet now?"

"She's with her mother," Lucy told her.

Vonk came shooting out of his butler's pantry, a copy of the latest *Penny Dreadful* clutched in his hand. He'd clearly been having a sneaky break while everyone else was working.

"Whatever's wrong, Mrs C?"

"The girls were attacked! Violet's been hurt, but don't worry – she's safely at home now."

"What?" Vonk dropped the *Penny*. He took one look at Lucy and said, "Mrs Crawley, a pot of hot, strong tea is in order, I think."

"Right you are! Becky, get that kettle boiling."

"You'll have to do it! I need to pick all this up!"

Becky said. She was down on her hands and knees, scrabbling about for her spilled beans.

While Mrs Crawley clattered around making tea, Vonk sat down opposite Lucy. "What happened?" he asked.

Lucy shakily explained everything, or almost everything. Becky was in earshot, under the table picking up stray beans, so she didn't mention that she'd used magic to defend Violet.

"And you're not hurt?" Vonk asked when she'd finished.

"No."

"Here you are – this has plenty of sugar in it." Mrs Crawley put a cup of tea in front of Lucy.

"Thanks." Lucy blew on the tea and then took a sip. It was hot, sweet and very comforting, and she began to recover a little.

By now Becky had finished picking up the beans and sat back down at the table. She took another pod and resumed her shelling in silence. Lucy noticed Becky's hands were trembling. Becky always made a point of being horrible to Violet, but the attack on

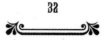

the poor little scullery maid seemed to have genuinely upset her.

"I think I'd better go and see Lord Grave and tell him what happened. He'll want to know," Lucy said when she'd finished her tea and felt a little more like her usual self.

"Don't worry, I'll explain it all to him," Vonk said.

Lucy glanced at Becky, who luckily seemed distracted by her beans, then shook her head gently at Vonk. He immediately understood that there was something more Lucy needed to tell Lord Grave, and it couldn't be said in front of Becky.

"On second thoughts, perhaps it might be best if you hurry along and speak to his Lordship yourself. I've got a lot to do."

As she left the kitchen, Lucy glanced over her shoulder and caught Becky staring at her. Their eyes met for a second before Becky swiftly diverted her gaze back to her bowl of beans. In that second, Lucy realised that the normally abrasive under-housemaid was not simply upset by what had happened to Violet; she was frightened.

CHAPTER FOUR

THE BLOODY PENNY

"I'm really sorry. I know I shouldn't have used the attack sparks. I did it without thinking," Lucy said, when she'd finished explaining the morning's events to Lord Grave. She was sitting in one of the green wing-backed armchairs next to the fire in the drawing room.

"There's nothing to be sorry for. You probably saved Violet's life," Lord Grave replied. He was sitting in the chair opposite Lucy's. Bathsheba lay near him, snoozing in front of the fire. Her mouth

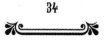

was partly open, the gleaming points of her fangs on display, and she was dribbling rather gracelessly on to the green woollen hearthrug.

"But what if I'm right and the boy saw the sparks as well as felt them?"

"I suppose he might say something to any accomplices he might have, but he's not likely to go to the authorities to report anything suspicious, is he?"

"Could he have been a magician?"

"Hmm. I know all the magicians in the area, young and old. I don't recognise him from your description. It's possible, though, that he might have come from somewhere else."

"I wonder what he wanted? Why would he bother attacking a servant girl like Violet? He must have realised she wouldn't have jewellery or anything like that. And she'd already given him threepence, all the money she had on her," Bertie said, picking absentmindedly at the frayed material that covered the footstool he was perched on. Bathsheba had a bad habit of using it to sharpen her claws on.

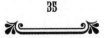

"That's a good point, my boy." Lord Grave took a puff of his cigar, which was unlit as he was trying to give them up. Or at least he was when Bertie was around. "Lucy, is there anything more you remember that might give us a clue?"

Lucy thought carefully. "There is something that I don't understand. Just before the boy ran off, he said something about Caruthers. Something like 'that stupid frog' . . . Why would he say that?"

"Where was Caruthers at the time?" Bertie asked.

"He was on the ground. I dropped him."

"*You* dropped him? When the boy attacked you and Violet, who was holding Caruthers?"

"Me."

Bertie leaned forward, his dark bushy eyebrows drawn together in a thoughtful frown. "Did the boy say anything else?"

"Yes. Something like . . . 'you're her'. He seemed quite confused." Lucy replied, remembering how the boy had looked from her to Violet and back again. "Maybe . . . maybe he thought I was Violet because I was holding Caruthers?"

36

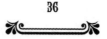

"And maybe he thought Violet was you!" Bertie said excitedly. "Which means he meant to attack you first."

"It's a good theory, my boy," Lord Grave said. "But it still leaves us with the same question. Why would anyone want to attack Lucy? We need to speak to little Violet in case she saw anything that might provide a clue as to the boy's motive. Lucy, you go and rest for an hour, then we'll visit Violet. In the meantime I'll ask Vonk to ready the carriage."

＊

Half an hour later, Lucy was lying on her brass bed in the little attic room she shared with Becky. She felt too keyed up to nap. Bored of staring at the ceiling, she got off the bed and went over to the window. One of the few good points about her bedroom, which was so small the door opened outwards instead of inwards to save space, was the view of Lord Grave's wildlife park. Lord Grave's wife had been an animal lover. When she was alive, she had made a habit of rescuing animals: anything from birds to elephants.

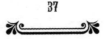

Lord Grave had recently employed extra help to care for the animals. That extra help could be seen lumbering about now, carrying meat for the lions. Lucy smiled as she watched the golem going about its duties. It had been her idea to make the golem a wildlife park keeper. Of course, the creation of golems was a strictly forbidden type of magic. A rogue magician called Jerome Wormwood had brought this particular one to life just a few weeks ago. Thanks to Lucy, Wormwood was now safely locked up and wouldn't be creating any more monsters for a very long time. However, that had left MAAM with the problem of what to do with the golem, who was now harmless, thanks to some vigorous retraining, but still somewhat alarming.

Realising that humans, especially anyone non-magical, might be rather disturbed by the golem, Lord Grave had put a special shielding spell on it. This meant that its true form could be seen only by MAAM associates and the magical residents of Grave Hall. Anyone else would see a rather portly, unkempt, slightly smelly man who went by the name of Mr Gomel. This all worked well enough, although care had to be taken to make sure no one tried to engage Mr Gomel in meaningful conversation, as that might give the game away.

As she gazed out at the wildlife park, watching some pelicans flying around the lake, Lucy went over the attack again in her mind. She frowned as she remembered that when the boy had tumbled off Violet and on to his back he'd dropped something and then quickly snatched it up again. Lucy closed her eyes and gripped the edge of the windowsill. She concentrated as hard as she could, trying to visualise again what she'd seen. The boy's hand reaching out to grab the object. What was it? But it was no good – she couldn't bring it to mind. Perhaps Violet would be able to remember something more. Eager to find out, Lucy hurriedly left her little attic room and set off downstairs to meet Lord Grave.

*

The Worthingtons' cottage lay a little way outside Grave Village, up a narrow lane. The cottage was

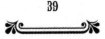

small but well cared for. Lord Grave rapped the shiny brass knocker. A moment later, Mrs Worthington opened it.

"Your Lordship!" she said, looking most surprised and also not very pleased.

"I'm very sorry to intrude, but I wondered if we could have a quick word with Violet."

Mrs Worthington frowned. "Oh dear. Can't it wait? The poor little thing's worn out. She can hardly keep her eyes open."

"Just a few minutes?"

Mrs Worthington sighed. "If you insist."

"Most kind." Lord Grave took off his top hat and stepped through the doorway. Lucy followed him inside.

The cottage had just one large room downstairs. The floorboards were bare, but swept clean. Not a speck of dust clung to the rough wooden beams that crossed the ceiling. Mrs Worthington led the way up the rickety staircase, which creaked rather alarmingly.

The stairs opened out directly on to a bedroom that was as small as Lucy's own but seemed bigger

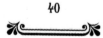

as there was only the one bed, which Violet was lying in. She and Caruthers were snugly tucked up under a pink-and-white patchwork quilt.

Mrs Worthington bent over her daughter and spoke gently to her. "Violet. Lord Grave's here. He wants to speak to you. Is that all right?"

"Yes, Mother," Violet said. Her voice was slow and sleepy.

Mrs Worthington gestured for Lord Grave and Lucy to go over to Violet's bed.

"Hello, Lucy. Thank you for saving me," Violet said. She looked up at her two visitors. Her eyes were dull and her face looked pinched and grey.

"Violet, I'd just like you to tell me what you remember of the attack. The boy cut you with his knife, is that right?" Lord Grave said kindly.

Violet nodded.

"And then what happened?"

Violet's eyes began to close. "A penny. Then a peashooter," she whispered.

"I think she's delirious," Lord Grave muttered.

Violet's eyes opened a little. "The boy. He cut me.

41

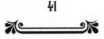

He had a penny. Smeared it with my blood. Put it in his handkerchief. Then Lucy hit him on the back of the neck with her peashooter. Can I go to sleep now?"

Lord Grave opened his mouth to ask another question, but Mrs Worthington stepped between him and the bed. "I think that's enough for today, sir," she said firmly, and began ushering Lucy and Lord Grave towards the stairs. Lucy glanced over her shoulder and saw that Violet was already fast asleep.

When Lord Grave and Lucy had been politely but speedily shown out of the Worthingtons' cottage, Lord Grave lingered on the doorstep for a few moments.

"I wish I could have gleaned a little more information from young Violet. I'm beginning to think your attacker really might have been magical."

Lucy frowned. "If he was, why didn't he use magic to fight back when I hit him with the attack sparks?"

Lord Grave nodded. "That's a good point. But perhaps he'd already got what he wanted? Which in this case was blood. Perhaps he'd hoped for *your* blood, but decided to make do with Violet's."

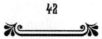

"But why would he do such a thing?" Lucy asked, feeling slightly queasy.

Lord Grave put his top hat back on and gazed grimly at Lucy. "There are many magical uses for blood, Lucy, and all of them are very nasty indeed."

CHAPTER FIVE

LORD PERCY AND THE CUSTARD SLICE

Back at Grave Hall, Lucy expected that she and Lord Grave would spend some time together discussing what Violet had revealed. But Lord Grave had other ideas.

"It's a stroke of luck that I invited MAAM to come a couple of days before the actual ball so that we could have a catch-up before the other guests arrive. Lord Percy sent me a chit this morning to let me know they'd all be here at five."

Lucy, who had become more and more acquainted with the magical world over the last few weeks, knew that chits were a special invention of Lord Percy's; flying notes that MAAM used to send messages between themselves, and to communicate with other magicians.

"So," Lord Grave continued, consulting his pocket watch, "there's about half an hour before they arrive. We'll be able to confer with them about all this later. In the meantime, would you mind helping Mrs Crawley? I believe she may be feeling somewhat overwhelmed with the preparations for the ball."

Lucy agreed, but she couldn't help feeling a little put out. Sometimes she resented the fact that Lord Grave wanted her to be part of MAAM, but also expected her to be a servant. Nevertheless, she set off to the kitchen.

Mrs Crawley was sitting at the kitchen table, surrounded by a stack of potatoes. She was sipping at a large tankard of her favourite home-brew. The ale was flavoured with Extra Violent Mustard Mix and Mrs Crawley used it as a pick-me-up when she was feeling particularly fatigued.

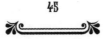

"Oh, thank goodness!" she said when she saw Lucy. "I really do need a hand! All these potatoes need peeling, could you make a start on them? Becky keeps sneaking off somewhere. She's acting very oddly. Lord Percy and the rest of MAAM are arriving soon. Oh, and Diamond O'Brien and the rest of the circus folk are coming tomorrow. It's all going to be a bit frantic now until the big day!"

"Have you ever seen the circus?" Lucy asked, picking up a potato and starting to peel it. Lord Grave had invited O'Brien's Midnight Circus to provide some entertainment at the ball. Lucy had seen some of the acts before, and had been extremely impressed.

"No, his Lordship hasn't always approved of that sort of thing," Mrs Crawley said, taking a gulp of her ale.

This was true. Relations between MAAM and O'Brien's Midnight Circus had been somewhat glacial due to the fact that the circus folk operated on what Lord Grave called "the fringes of ethical magic". However, following the death of two magicians at the hands of Jerome Wormwood, Lord

Grave and Diamond O'Brien had decided that the magical community needed to come together.

"Oh, you'll love it! There's magical knife-throwing, a woman who can fold herself up and trapeze artists. Without trapezes!"

"That sounds very exciting, to be sure!" Mrs Crawley wiped beery foam from her moustache. The refreshment had rallied her and she recovered her usual good spirits. "Now then. Lord Grave wants to give MAAM a nice dinner tonight. I'd like you and Becky to wait at table, Lucy. Don't pull that face. If the wind changes you'll be stuck like that. You and Becky need to work together sometimes."

Lucy sighed inwardly, but decided not to argue. She carried on peeling potatoes. "How are MAAM getting here?" she asked after a while.

"They're all coming in Lady Sibyl's coach." Mrs Crawley glanced at the kitchen clock. "They should be here any minute."

"Can I go and watch them land?"

Mrs Crawley smiled. "Of course. Off you go, but don't be too long."

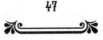

"Thank you!" Lucy jumped out of her seat, raced out of the back door and through the kitchen garden. Watching Lady Sibyl's flying coach arrive was always a thrill. Lucy had ridden in it herself once and dearly hoped she'd do so again one day.

When she reached the front of the house, she stood on the gravel driveway and gazed upwards. She soon spotted an unusual black smudge in the sky. There was a rumbling noise like faint thunder as the smudge grew bigger and bigger, and after a few seconds Lucy could clearly see Lady Sibyl's shiny black carriage, which was pulled by two horses whose gossamer-thin wings shimmered with rainbow colours where the autumn sunlight touched them.

Lucy skittered out of the coach's flight path and watched from a safe distance as it began to lose height, landing with a gentle crunch on the Grave drive. The coach driver, a slender woman dressed from head to toe in black velvet, deftly pulled the horses to a halt.

Behind Lucy, the grand front door of Grave Hall opened, and Lord Grave and Bathsheba came down the steps. Bertie and Vonk followed. Lucy eagerly ran

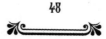

up to the coach, preparing to greet her fellow MAAM members.

The stout footman travelling alongside the driver jumped down and hurried over to pull out the carriage steps so the passengers could disembark. Then he unfastened the door and held it open as Lady Sibyl started climbing out.

"Hello!" Lucy called excitedly. But her greeting wasn't returned.

Lady Sibyl was frowning distractedly. Usually, she was very elegant and sure-footed, but not today, as she stumbled on the last of the coach steps and had to be steadied by her footman. The cause of her upset soon became clear when Beguildy Beguildy and his sister Prudence followed her, helping Lord Percy out of the coach. Lucy gasped and put her hand over her mouth. Poor Lord Percy, who was a sorrowful-looking man at the best of times, was in a terrible state and looked more miserable than ever. His right arm was in a sling, his left eye was swollen and turning black and he had a very nasty cut on his cheek, which was clotted with dried blood.

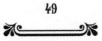

"What on earth happened to you, old chap?" Lord Grave boomed, striding over to Lord Percy, who was now wearily leaning against Beguildy's shoulder.

"We stopped off in Grave Village on the way here. I had a fancy for one of Busby's custard slices. You know how fond I am of them. I was attacked by two blasted urchins. A girl and a boy. Unbelievable," Lord Percy replied.

"Did they steal anything?" Lord Grave asked.

"No. Managed to fight the little guttersnipes off. Left me with a few cuts and bruises, that's all,"

"A few cuts and bruises! Dear Percy was very lucky, George. The boy had a knife." Lady Sibyl's words gave Lucy a little jolt, and she exchanged glances with Lord Grave, who was surely thinking the same thing as her – was this the same boy who'd attacked her and Violet?

"The vicious little beast wielded it without hesitation, and he would have used it on me if Percy hadn't bravely shielded me from harm," Lady Sibyl continued, dabbing at her eyes with a very fancy lace

handkerchief. "But you know the most disturbing thing of all, George? Those beastly children weren't just ordinary nasty little reprobates. They were magical."

CHAPTER SIX

HARD TIMES HALL

L ord Grave raised his bushy eyebrows.
"Extraordinary. Come on, Percy, let's get you
inside and comfortable, then you can tell all.
Vonk, would you organise tea in the MAAM
meeting room please? Lucy, perhaps you could help
Vonk and then join us."

Lord Grave and Beguildy each grabbed one of
Lord Percy's elbows and began to guide him up the
steps to the front door and into the hallway of the
house. Once everyone was inside, Lord Percy, Lady

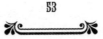

Sibyl and the Beguildys removed their coats and hats. After warming themselves in front of the hallway fire, they headed off to the MAAM meeting room with Lord Grave, leaving Lucy and Vonk to lug all the outdoor garments to the coat cupboard.

"Children attacking you and Violet, and now Lord Percy!" Vonk shook his head as he hung up Lady Sibyl's cloak, which was trimmed with black and scarlet feathers.

"I'd bet my life one of them is the boy from the alley," Lucy replied, reaching up to hang Beguildy Beguildy's navy-blue coat, which had a very fancy brass neck-fastening featuring a ship in full sail.

"We'll soon find out. No doubt MAAM will get to the bottom of it. Come along, we'd best go and fetch the tea things."

When Lucy and Vonk reached the kitchen, Vonk looked cautiously around before asking where Becky was.

Mrs Crawley gave a little snort of amusement. "Cleaning out the lavatories and the chamber pots. I know I shouldn't laugh. She's absolutely furious, but

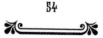

with Violet laid up . . . Whatever's the matter, Vonk?"

"There's been another incident, Mrs C." Vonk pulled out a chair and sat at the table. Lucy and Mrs Crawley did likewise. Then Vonk explained what had happened to Lord Percy and Lady Sibyl in Grave Village.

"But that's terrible," Mrs Crawley said when Vonk had finished speaking. "Poor Lord Percy. Could there be some connection to the attack on Violet and Lucy? What does his Lordship think?"

"I haven't had a chance to ask him, but *I* think there is," Lucy told her. "He's having a MAAM meeting now. He asked for some tea to be sent up. We'd better put plenty of sugar in Lord Percy's."

"Oh, but of course!" Mrs Crawley immediately began buzzing around the kitchen, putting the kettle to boil on the range and setting out the china on a tray, as well as a couple of plates of biscuits. While Mrs Crawley was attending to the teapot, Lucy and Vonk swiftly examined the biscuits. They were relieved to find that they were normal almond ones without any experimental flourishes such as cockroach legs.

When everything was ready, they set off upstairs.

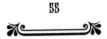

Vonk carried the tea tray and Lucy carried the biscuit plates.

"You can do the honours, Lucy," Vonk said when the two of them reached the door to the MAAM meeting room.

"Havana!" Lucy exclaimed. She always enjoyed being the one to utter the password that made the meeting-room door swing open of its own accord. And, although she was now quite familiar with what lay beyond the door, she still felt a buzz of excitement at stepping over the threshold and into such a fascinating room. A large glass display cabinet took up the whole of one wall, and it was filled with strange-looking instruments made of silver, gold and brass. They were all inventions created by Lord Percy and had various uses, including detecting the misuse of magic. At the moment, all of them were silent and still.

"You should settle yourself down with the others and I'll serve the tea," Vonk whispered to Lucy.

As Vonk busied himself with pouring tea and handing round the biscuits (Lucy smiled to herself as she saw that each member of MAAM examined

them suspiciously before eating them), Lucy parked herself next to Bertie and Smell.

"I call this meeting to order!" Lord Grave announced. "In light of what happened to Lord Percy today, we need to consider who the children behind the attack might be. Sibyl, Percy, what made you conclude your attackers were magical? Did they cast any spells?"

"Briefly," Lady Sibyl said. "The boy tried. He very clumsily aimed some attack sparks at me when I went to Percy's aid."

At that very moment, the glass cabinet began to rattle. One of the instruments, a golden star attached to a coiled golden spring, was bouncing up and down.

"Why is it doing that?" Lucy asked.

"Because somewhere a child is using magic, or rather using magic when they shouldn't," Lord Grave explained. "You see, although child magicians can of course use magic, it's generally not allowed unless they are in their own home or another magician's home and are being supervised by an adult. There's simply too much that could go wrong. This little contraption gives the alert if a child is breaking the rules. Of course they could be clever enough to make their magic undetectable, but they would have to be exceptionally talented."

The golden star began jiggling even more wildly.

"Can it tell you who's doing the magic? Or where?" Lucy asked.

Lord Grave shook his head. "It covers a radius of some two hundred miles, but it can't pin down an exact location or identify the culprit. But I would wager that it has something to do with today's events. The last time that machine went off on a regular basis was a couple of months ago, when you were being a little wayward with magic, Lucy. That's what set me off looking for you."

Lucy felt her face grow warm. When she'd first met Lord Grave, she'd been using a magical playing card to win poker games, although at the time she had thought it was simply some sort of trick card. Lord Grave had brought her to Grave Hall so that she could learn to use magic properly.

Her embarrassment increased when Beguildy

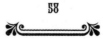

Beguildy made an exaggerated tutting noise and wagged his forefinger in an admonishing manner. Lucy and Beguildy weren't exactly the best of friends. However, he had rescued her from a stressful situation during the Jerome Wormwood investigation, so now she was trying to be a little more tolerant of him and vice versa. Admittedly, this could be a challenge at times on both sides.

"Let's get back to business," Lord Grave continued. "Percy, Sibyl, can you describe the children who attacked you?"

"I didn't get a good look at them," Lady Sibyl said. "Percy?"

Lord Percy grunted and opened his eyes. He'd been nodding off, his head drooping towards the table. "Sorry, what?"

"The children. Can you describe them?" Lord Grave said.

"Oh, well. Let me think. The girl wore a cloak. Hood up. Couldn't see her face. The boy . . . Tattoo on his neck, under his ear. Looked like a bluebird." Lord Percy's head began to droop again.

"A tattoo?" Lord Grave said. He puffed excitedly on his unlit cigar. "We could have a lead here. Do you all remember the Hard Times Hall fiasco?"

"Hard Times Hall! Yes, you could be on to something, George," Lady Sibyl said, nodding her head vigorously. The peacock feathers she wore in her hair bobbed up and down as if in agreement.

"What's Hard Times Hall?" Lucy asked.

"An orphanage for magical children. Wait a moment." Lord Grave left the table and went over to a large wooden chest. He lifted the lid to reveal a mass of papers inside. Although they looked rather haphazard, they must have been in some sort of order as Lord Grave soon managed to locate what he needed. He pulled out some newspaper pages. They were slightly yellowed and when Lucy looked closely she saw they were from an edition of the *Penny Dreadful* and dated the year before. Lord Grave always called the *Penny* a "frightful old rag" but nevertheless he seemed to be one of its most loyal readers and had an extensive collection of back copies. Lord Grave spread the pages in front of Lucy and Bertie.

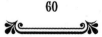

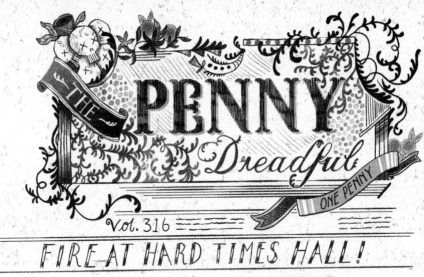

PENNY
Dreadful

ONE PENNY

Vol. 316

FIRE AT HARD TIMES HALL!

FIRE BROKE OUT over the weekend at Hard Times Hall, the orphanage rumoured to be owned by Lord Grave. Although the fire was minor and soon quenched, it is believed that a number of orphans escaped and are still on the run. A keen-eyed resident witnessed some of the escapees, and an artist's impression of them is shown above.

"You own an orphanage, Father?" Bertie asked in astonishment.

Lord Grave waved his hand dismissively. "As far as the *Penny* and the rest of the non-magical world is concerned, I do. But in truth it belongs to the whole of the magical community. It's where we look after magical children who have no one else to care for them. But all that's by the by. The point here is those children who escaped. About a dozen of 'em, have never been found. Or perhaps not found until now."

Lord Grave pointed at the drawings of the Hard Times Hall escapees. "Percy, this boy with curly hair, he has a bluebird tattoo on his neck, do you see? Is it the same boy?"

Lord Percy had to be prodded awake by Beguildy Beguildy. He stared intently at the drawings that accompanied the article, as though he was finding it difficult to focus. "Yes. He looked a little older than he is here, but yes, that's him."

"Sibyl? Do you recognise the boy too? Or these other children?"

"As I said, I didn't manage more than a glimpse

of any of them. I was too concerned about dear Percy."

Lady Sibyl wasn't the only one to be concerned about dear Lord Percy. The rest of MAAM looked at him in alarm as he began swaying gently in his seat, as though being blown by an invisible wind, his eyes were closing again.

"Oh dear. I must admit I'm not feeling very well," he muttered.

"I think we'd better get you into a nice warm bed," Lord Grave said. "Vonk, is Lord Percy's room ready?"

Vonk stepped forward from the corner where he had been quietly standing. He often stayed on hand when there was a MAAM meeting going on, in case anything was needed. "Yes, I believe so."

"I would like a brief lie-down, I must admit," Lord Percy said. He tried to stand up, but it was clear that he wasn't going to be able to make it out of the room and up the stairs to bed under his own steam. Vonk hurried off to fetch Mrs Crawley, who soon bore Lord Percy away upstairs to bed in her strong and beefy arms.

"Lucy, you need to have a good look at these drawings too," Lord Grave said when everyone had settled down again and the meeting had resumed. "Could any of them be the boy who attacked you and Violet?"

"You were attacked too? Oh, Lucy, how horrid for you!" Prudence Beguildy exclaimed.

"Who's Violet?" Beguildy asked.

"Isn't that the little scullery maid? The one with the green frog?" Prudence Beguildy asked. "Such a sweet girl! I hope she wasn't hurt?"

"She's got a nasty cut on her hand," Lucy replied, and then told the rest of MAAM about the attack and the bloody penny.

"The poor little thing!" Prudence said when Lucy had finished her story.

"Could it have been one of these orphans, Lucy?" Lord Grave asked.

Lucy peered at the drawings. "Maybe the boy with curly hair. I didn't notice he had a tattoo, but his face and neck were dirty, so maybe it was hidden?"

Lord Grave nodded. "Yes, that's a possibility."

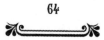

"But why would a magician, even a child magician, bother attacking a non-magical scullery maid?" Beguildy suddenly piped up. "Why would they even notice such a person?"

Lucy bristled at Beguildy's snobbish tone. He obviously thought the only thing lower than a servant was a non-magical servant. She opened her mouth to say something, but then closed it, remembering their truce. She'd faithfully promised Lord Grave that she would try her hardest not to break it.

"It's a good question, Beguildy, if somewhat harshly put." Lord Grave narrowed his eyes, thinking deeply. "However, we think it might have been an error on the attacker's part, and he was actually targeting Lucy."

"Same question applies," Beguildy said, examining his nails.

"Stop it, B," Prudence said.

"Quite," Lady Sibyl said. "Lucy is one of us now."

"I think it's possible that the two incidents could be linked," Lord Grave mused. "Whether Hard Times Hall really has any bearing on the case . . .

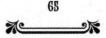

Well, my view is that we should keep an open mind about that for now."

*

When the meeting was over, Lucy helped Vonk carry the tea things back to the kitchen. The room was now so full of steam that it was barely possible to see. Mrs Crawley's face suddenly loomed out of the haze, her beard sparkling with tiny droplets from the damp air. "Oh no, not MORE washing-up!"

"Where's Becky?" Vonk asked, carefully making his way to the only-just-visible table to deposit the tea tray.

"Oh, she's fussing about cleaning her uniform for this evening. I think she might have spilled a chamber pot down herself. She's in a very strange mood. Seems rather upset about Violet. Keeps asking me if we've had any more news about her."

"I'm sure you can handle her, Mrs C. Right then. I need to finish polishing the silver ready for tonight," Vonk said. Seizing the opportunity to make a break for some steam-free air, he scuttled into his butler's pantry and closed the door.

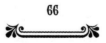

"That's a great help, I must say!" Mrs Crawley snapped.

"I'll do the dishes," Lucy offered.

"Oh, thank you! I don't mean to be so grumpy – it's just all too much for me at the moment." Mrs Crawley took out a very large white handkerchief embroidered with purple flowers and wiped her face with it.

Lucy went through to the scullery, where the steamy haze was lighter. Mrs Crawley brought in the huge black kettle from the range and filled the sink with hot water. She cast a cautious look over her shoulder and then said, "I have to say, I sometimes question his Lordship's decision to employ non-magical servants."

"What do you mean?" Lucy added soap flakes to the water and began swishing them around.

"Of course I'm very fond of Violet and, er, Becky. But life would be so much easier if I could use a little more of my magic day-to-day. It would cut down on the drudgery. But of course I can't. The girls are young yet, so we can't be sure they wouldn't see.

That's why his Lordship decided neither of them should be here for the actual ball."

"I've always wondered *why* Lord Grave hired Becky and Violet in the first place." Lucy asked, beginning to carefully wash up the cups and saucers.

"Well, you see, it's conventional for a big house to hire at least some of its staff from the local district. And you know Lord Grave is a very traditional man in many ways. But I do so wish he could break free of his traditions sometimes!"

✳

The Grave Hall dining room was very impressive, with its sparkling chandelier and the dozens of candles that hung on the wood-panelled walls. Lucy had helped serve dinner to MAAM once before, during her first few days at the Hall. That had only been a couple of months ago, but it seemed much longer than that to Lucy, as she'd had so many adventures since then. The meal that time had involved a bewitched chicken that had more body parts than normal, which had mystified

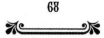

Lucy no end. But tonight there was no magical food. Mrs Crawley had thought it too risky because of Becky.

"Right, girls," whispered Vonk. Along with Lucy and Becky, he was at the mahogany sideboard where all the food for his Lordship's guests was laid out, including an array of desserts. "Lucy, you carry the lamb; Becky, you serve it up. Make sure you do the ladies first."

Vonk handed Lucy a large silver platter on which he had carefully arranged the slices of lamb he'd carved, and then drizzled them with mint sauce. Becky was given a pair of ornate silver tongs.

Lucy carefully carried the platter of lamb to the table. "Lamb, Lady Sibyl?"

Lady Sibyl shook her head. "Not for me. I'm not very hungry."

"Oh, come now, Sibyl," Lord Grave boomed. "You need to eat!"

Lady Sibyl smiled weakly. "Very well. Just a small slice."

Lucy and Becky worked their way round the table

with the lamb. Lady Sibyl's appetite might have been subdued by the day's events, but Beguildy Beguildy's was completely untroubled.

"Another slice. Yes, another slice. Just one more," he kept saying until the platter had to go back to the sideboard, where Vonk refilled it with freshly carved slices and more mint sauce.

"Quickly now, girls." Vonk whispered. "Serve Lord Grave before everything gets cold."

Lucy carried the platter over to the head of the table where Lord Grave was sitting. For some reason, Becky had left her tongs on the sideboard and was instead using Vonk's carving knife to manoeuvre meat on to Lord Grave's plate. She was being very clumsy about it and suddenly lost her grip on the knife, dropping it blade down towards Lord Grave's hand. As he was busy trying to cheer up Lady Sibyl, he didn't realise what was happening.

"Look out!" Lucy warned, accidentally tilting the platter. Lamb and mint sauce spilled over Lord Grave's shoulder and onto the floor.

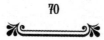

"What on earth!" Lord Grave leaped from his seat. The blade of the knife grazed the side of his little finger before twanging into the table.

"Oh, sir! Your hand! It's bleeding!" Becky whipped a handkerchief from her apron pocket and attempted to wipe the tiny spots of blood from the small scratch the knife had caused.

"Never mind my hand – this is my best dinner jacket!" Lord Grave snatched the handkerchief from Becky and used it to dab at the grease and mint sauce that was soaking into his shoulder. Bathsheba, who had been lying under the table, added to the confusion by careering around, snatching up pieces of fallen lamb and wolfing them down.

By now, Vonk had rushed over to Lord Grave. "I'm so sorry, your Lordship. Thank goodness Lucy acted so swiftly! Becky, what in heaven's name were you doing using the carving knife in that way? What happened to the tongs?"

"You should have been supervising the girl more closely, Vonk! Oh, Lucy, please stop Bathsheba

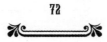

guzzling! Mint sauce doesn't agree with her stomach at all!"

Lucy pulled at Bathsheba's jewelled collar in an attempt to drag her away from the meat. The panther turned and roared ferociously, obviously forgetting that she and Lucy were supposedly on good terms. Food before friendship was clearly her philosophy. As Lucy didn't fancy sacrificing a limb to save Bathsheba from a tummy upset, she hastily backed away. Behind her, Beguildy was making his way to the sideboard for seconds, having calmly finished his pile of lamb despite the upheaval going on. Lucy banged into him and he lost his footing before landing face first in one of Mrs Crawley's immensely tall and wobbly trifles.

It took a good while for order to be restored and by that time all the food had gone cold. Lord Grave decided to abandon dinner and instead ordered sandwiches to be served in the drawing room. Lucy and the other servants worked flat out to clear up the mess in the dining room as well as make everyone comfortable in the drawing room. The MAAM members soon settled down, except for Beguildy

Beguildy, who was developing a nasty black eye from hitting his cheek against the edge of the cut-glass trifle bowl and was determined to make the most of his injuries.

"I could have lost an eye! That butler of yours should be sacked for allowing dim housemaids to run riot with knives!" Lucy heard him raging when she served coffee to the guests. She felt like poking him in the other eye with the sugar tongs.

When Lucy finally escaped back down to the kitchen, she found that Becky had gone to bed early, apparently completely distraught at almost stabbing Lord Grave's hand. Lucy suspected she'd really nabbed the chance to get out of doing the washing up. As for Vonk, he was terribly upset at the way Lord Grave had blamed him for the incident and was refusing to be comforted even by Mrs Crawley's offer of a calming glass of her home-made spinach brandy.

CHAPTER SEVEN

THE WAR OF THE MAIDS

When Lucy yawned her way down to the kitchen the next morning, she was surprised to find Violet there, already clearing away the breakfast things. Lucy managed to swipe a couple of pieces of toast before everything was put away.

"I didn't think you'd be here today! Are you all right?" She gave Violet a quick hug. The difference in the little scullery maid was astounding. Yesterday she'd looked grim, grey-faced and barely awake.

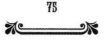

Today her eyes sparkled and her cheeks were rosy.

"Oh yes, I'm fine now!" Violet replied, squirming out of Lucy's arms.

"Convenient, that. Now that all the smelly cleaning jobs have been done," snapped Becky, who was sitting at the table with Mrs Crawley, drinking a cup of tea. Becky looked as unwell as Violet had yesterday; there were shadows under her eyes and her blonde hair was shoved messily under her cap. This was strange as Becky was usually very particular about her hair. Lucy wasn't surprised to see her looking ill, though. She'd heard her tossing and turning in the night and even talking in her sleep.

"Oh, shut up!" Violet retorted. She picked up a rind of bacon from one of the plates she was clearing and threw it at Becky. The bacon bounced off Becky's cap then landed on the floor. Smell suddenly appeared from nowhere and gulped the bacon rind down before anyone could stop him.

"Violet, really!" Mrs Crawley said. "What's got into you?"

"There's a grease stain on my cap! You little . . ."

Becky sprang out of her chair and grabbed Violet by the hair. Violet retaliated by grasping Becky's ear and twisting it. They fell against the table, upsetting the pile of plates, which crashed to the stone floor and smashed into pieces. Smell began snuffling around the shards, no doubt in search of a tasty morsel or two, but he soon had to scoot out of the way to avoid being trodden on by the two warring maids.

"Stop this at once!" bellowed Mrs Crawley. "Vonk! Help!"

Vonk darted out of the butler's pantry and stood for a few seconds, aghast at the scene before him. Then he made a beeline for Becky, grabbing her by the collar, while Mrs Crawley did the same with Violet. Once they had been separated, the two girls stood glaring at each other.

Smell jumped up on to the kitchen table. "Vi looks proper aggrieved," he said to Lucy, speaking very quietly so no one else could hear. He was right. Violet was standing in a very un-Violet like way, feet apart, hands balled up into fists.

"This isn't like you, Violet!" Vonk was saying.

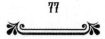

"Too right it isn't," Becky spat. "She's usually so namby pamby and weedy. *Namby pamby and weedy.*"

Violet started and her eyes widened as though she'd just remembered something very important. She relaxed her fists. "I-I'm sorry, Becky. I shouldn't have thrown that bacon at you. I don't know what came over me."

Mrs Crawley put her hands on her hips and scowled. "That's more like it. Becky?"

"Are you going to make her buy me a new cap?" Becky demanded.

"Becky!" Mrs Crawley said in a warning manner.

"Oh, all right, I'm sorry too," Becky said, rushing the words out.

"Shake hands," Vonk ordered, looking every bit as stern as Mrs Crawley did. The two maids almost did as they were told. They very briefly touched palms, not looking at each other as they did so.

"Well, that's a start, I suppose," Mrs Crawley said with a sigh. "Now we really must get on. We need to get as much done as possible before Diamond O'Brien and the rest of the circus folk arrive. Lucy,

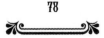

I want you to clean the windows at the front of the house. They're filthy."

"Good idea, Mrs C. We don't want his Lordship's visitors thinking we neglect the Hall," Vonk said. "You get the cleaning utensils, Lucy, and I'll . . . um . . . get the ladders sent round."

As Vonk left the kitchen he winked at Mrs Crawley, who chuckled a little, although Lucy wasn't sure why. Then the housekeeper-cum-cook rummaged around in the cupboard where all the cleaning things were kept. She handed Lucy a bottle of vinegar mixed with water, and some scrunched-up newspaper. Then she turned to Violet and Becky.

"I want you two to make a start on cleaning the bedrooms in the east wing. I'll be along to check up on you, mind. Any sort of fracas and you'll both be answering to his Lordship. Use the servants' staircase, I don't want you bumping into any of the guests."

Neither Becky nor Violet replied, but they grabbed some cleaning things and headed towards the door at the side of the kitchen, which led to the servants' staircase.

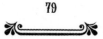

Lucy was about to go outside and make a start on the windows when she noticed Caruthers lying abandoned under the kitchen table with a scrap of fried egg stuck to his head. He must have fallen out of Violet's apron pocket when she and Becky were squaring up to each other.

"Violet! You forgot Caruthers," she called. Violet turned back and gazed at the woolly amphibian.

"Who? Oh yes. Thank you so much, Lucy. Poor old thing." Violet took the knitted frog from Lucy and stuffed him into her apron pocket. She didn't even bother to clean the egg off first.

✳

Lucy went round to the front of the house. She waited for a little while, but there was no sign of Vonk or the ladders. She decided to get on with cleaning the lower windows. Using the crumpled newspaper she applied the solution Mrs Crawley had given her to the window next to the front door. The strong smell of vinegar made her eyes water. Then she began polishing the window. Once she'd finished, she

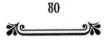

stepped back and was admiring her handiwork when she felt a strange prickle on the back of her neck, as though she was being watched. She turned round and saw that someone was indeed gazing intently at her. Someone with very long legs and an even longer neck. It was a giraffe from the wildlife park. Lucy bristled a little. She was certain the giraffe was the same one she'd had a confrontation with a few weeks ago.

"What are you doing here?" she asked.

Of course the giraffe didn't reply. It didn't seem to be planning to cause Lucy grief, however. In fact, it seemed to wink at her, batting its long eyelashes. Then it bent its neck, until its chin was almost on the ground. Lucy thought perhaps it had spotted some vegetation to nibble on, but the giraffe patiently stayed in position, its legs slightly splayed out in a rather comical fashion. Something was fluttering from one of its horns. It looked very much like a cleaning rag.

Lucy laughed with delight. The giraffe was the ladder Vonk had promised to send round! She gingerly climbed on to the creature's neck and held on to its horns as it lifted its head, carrying Lucy to the level of the first floor so that she could easily clean the windows. The giraffe seemed keen to help out by licking the glass with its blue tongue. To her great amusement, Lucy found that she could steer the giraffe using its horns. If she tugged gently on the left horn, the giraffe moved left, and vice versa.

Lucy manoeuvred the creature to the first-floor-landing windows. She'd just applied the vinegar mixture to them when she saw a blur of movement. Curious to see who it was, Lucy cleared a small patch of glass and peered through. Lord Percy was standing on the stairs, dressed in a white nightshirt and red plaid dressing gown. He wasn't alone. Becky was with him and the two of them seemed to be having a rather lively conversation. Lord Percy was pointing at Becky as if scolding her. Becky was halfway through making a rude gesture back when she seemed to sense someone was watching, and turned towards the window.

"Duck!" Lucy snapped instinctively.

Remarkably, the giraffe seemed to understand this command and lowered its neck so that the top of Lucy's head was just below the windowsill.

"Up a tiny bit so I can see what's going on," Lucy said quietly to the giraffe, which obliged. She was just in time to see Becky running off in the direction of the east wing. As for Lord Percy, he hunched himself up, clutched his head and began swaying as though he was about to faint. A moment later, Lord Grave came striding along the landing. He looked surprised to see Lord Percy out of bed. The two men had a short conversation, then Lord Grave took Lord Percy's arm and began steering him back towards his bedroom.

Lucy was perplexed. Why would Becky have been speaking to Lord Percy alone like that? And how could she dare to be so rude to him? Something odd was going on. She decided to investigate further.

"Would you mind moving to the left, towards the east wing?" she asked the giraffe. "But maybe keep your head down?"

The giraffe began shuffling left. As it made its way

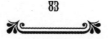

along, Lucy cautiously peered through each window, hoping to spot Becky. It wasn't until the giraffe reached the windows in the outer wall of the east-wing corridor that Lucy spied her. She wasn't alone – Violet was there too.

"Stop here, please," Lucy whispered to the giraffe.

The two housemaids were doing something very unexpected. They were tugging and rattling at the doorknob of a locked room. This was the Room of Curiosities, and Lucy had been inside it on a number of occasions and knew that it held many strange artefacts. Were Violet and Becky trying to break in and steal one of them? Lucy could believe Becky might do such a thing, but sweet, shy Violet? It seemed most unlikely. Obviously neither of them knew how to get inside the Room of Curiosities, but Lucy did. The statue of Lady Constance Grave, Lord Grave's great-grandmother, which stood outside in the corridor, guarded the keys. The only way to get hold of them was to tickle Lady Grave under the chin.

From the way they were gesticulating at each

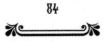

other, it was clear Violet and Becky were having yet another argument. Lucy tutted in frustration. If only she could hear what they were saying, she might be able to work out what they were up to! Then she noticed the handle of one window was slightly raised, meaning that it hadn't been shut properly from the inside. Lucy gingerly reached up and pushed at the window. It opened a little, enough for her to be able to hear the conversation.

"Why are you bothering?" Becky snapped. "You really think it's just going to unlock itself?"

"Well, it has to open somehow," Violet replied. "Are you certain it's in there?"

"Stop asking me that!" Becky exclaimed. "Like I told you, Goodly got in a few weeks ago. Then after that there was a day when half the house were in there. Crawley, Vonk, Grave, all of them. So I started keeping a close eye on it. I finally managed to get a glimpse inside when Grave went in a few days ago, and I'm sure I saw it. It's under a glass cover."

Violet gave the door a kick. "It's hopeless. If you'd been a bit sharper, Bone, you'd have realised months ago it was here. We'd have had more time to make a proper plan to get it."

"How could I have possibly known that, you idiot? I told you – I didn't even realise this room was here until I saw Lucy flaming Goodly going inside a few weeks ago."

"You're useless," Violet said, and rattled at the doorknob again.

Becky slapped at her hand. "Stop it, you're making too much noise."

Violet punched Becky on the arm. Lucy couldn't believe it. Sweet-natured, timid Violet wouldn't normally dare touch Becky, let alone fight with her twice in one morning! She fully expected Becky to retaliate and punch Violet right back, but she didn't. Instead, she said something that Lucy didn't catch, and then the two housemaids trotted out of sight round a corner.

"What was all that about?" Lucy said aloud. She decided to wait for a few minutes to see if Becky and Violet returned. After five minutes, Lucy was considering opening the window wider and climbing

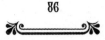

through to have a look around, when Becky came charging back along the corridor, her face screwed up in fury. She headed towards the stairs. A few seconds later, someone came running after her. Lucy nearly fell off her giraffe when she saw who it was.

The curly-haired boy with the bluebird neck tattoo who had ambushed her and Violet!

CHAPTER EIGHT

LORD GRAVE'S EXPLODING GREAT-GRANDMOTHER

Lucy was so astounded that for a few moments she couldn't move. Her brain scrambled to understand what she had just seen. Where was Violet? Had the boy done something to her? Why was she behaving so strangely? Lucy hesitated for a few seconds before deciding what to do next.

"Could you lift me up a bit higher, please?" she asked the giraffe. "I'm going inside for a minute, if you don't mind waiting for me here."

Lucy clambered through the window and jumped down into the now-deserted east-wing corridor. She scurried past the statue of Lady Constance Grave and the Room of Curiosities, and round the corner, in the direction she'd seen Becky and Violet go. There were a few spare bedrooms here, and she began carefully opening each door a crack and peering inside. There was no sign of Violet anywhere. Mystified, Lucy began to make her way back to the window where the giraffe would be patiently waiting. She was about to climb outside when that she noticed something floating along the corridor. It was a small web-like thread strung with tiny multi-coloured beads of moisture.

Lucy knew what it was at once – a trace of magic. She watched as it drifted along before vanishing in a flurry of sparks. The trace meant that someone had recently cast some sort of magic nearby. But neither Becky nor Violet were magical, so it must have been the boy she'd seen, which backed up Lord Grave's theory that he was a magical escapee from Hard Times Hall. But where had he gone? She hurriedly scrambled through the window and clambered on to the giraffe.

"Thanks very much for your help. I think we're finished with the window cleaning for today. Could you possibly let me down now?" The giraffe did as Lucy asked, bending its lengthy neck so that she could slide down to the ground. Then the two of them parted ways, Lucy heading for the kitchen while the giraffe lolloped off in the direction of the wildlife park.

✳

When Lucy reached the kitchen, she found it full of circus folk, drinking tea and eating biscuits.

"Lucy!" a young woman called.

Lucy hurried over to her. "Hello, Diamond!"

"How are you, my darling? I'm sure you've grown!" Diamond O'Brien, the owner of O'Brien's Midnight Circus, gave Lucy a warm hug. As usual, she was dressed in black satin offset by brightly coloured scarves. Her sleek dark hair was as short as ever, cut into sharp points round each ear.

"Good to see you, Lucy," said the man standing next to Diamond. He was very tall and wore an eye patch over his left eye. His beard was white with grey tips and was so long he wore the end thrown over his shoulder to keep it from dragging on the ground.

"Hello, Herbert," Lucy said, taking his outstretched hand and shaking it heartily

"We're so excited to be here," Diamond said. "We've got a treat of a display in store for this ball."

"I can't wait to see it!" Lucy replied.

Vonk came over to them. "Miss O'Brien! How lovely to see you again!"

Diamond smiled brightly. "Oh, Mr Vonk, do call me Diamond."

"You're so kind. I must say I'm terribly looking forward . . ."

While Vonk and Diamond were exchanging pleasantries, Lucy craned her neck, trying to see if Becky and the boy were anywhere to be seen. She quickly spotted Becky. Violet was with her. At least she was safe. But where was the boy? Lucy watched intently as the two maids weaved their way through the circus folk and slipped into the scullery, unnoticed by anyone else.

"Excuse me a second," Lucy said to Vonk and Diamond. Neither of them seemed to hear her, as they were too busy chatting and laughing. Lucy politely pushed her way through the throng of people to the scullery, stopping just outside.

"What a stupid thing to do! You're lucky no-one saw you!" Becky was saying.

"Oh, stop complaining for five seconds will you? Be grateful you don't have to wear one of the wretched things. It gets so *hot*. And smelly. I just wanted a break from it."

"Well, you won't need to use it for much longer. Valentina said once we find a way into that room, it'll all be over for Grave and the others."

"Shame you messed things up last night, Bone. You're lucky Grave didn't suspect anything," Violet said.

"Maybe I should try to take Goodly," Becky replied.

"You'd better ask Valentina first. Let's get out

of here. I want to find out what the plan is for tonight."

Lucy turned round to try to get out of sight as the two maids left the scullery. But the crowd was blocking her in and she couldn't shove her way through in time to avoid being seen.

"What are you lurking around for, Goodly?" Becky asked in her usual charming manner, narrowing her eyes.

"I wanted to ask you a question," Lucy said. She was about to mention the boy she'd seen, but then she hesitated, rapidly changing her plans. Perhaps she'd better pretend she hadn't seen him. There was obviously something suspicious going on and it seemed as though Becky and Violet might be involved, so it was probably better to keep quiet for now.

"Well?" Becky said, tapping her foot impatiently.

Lucy grinned desperately. "Isn't this all really exciting? I can't wait for the ball!"

"Oh, shut up, Goodly. I'm not even going to be here for the stupid ball. Why would I care anything about it?" Becky turned and stalked off, leaving

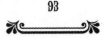

Violet and Lucy standing there, eyeing each other. Usually Violet would have said something sweet to counteract Becky's nastiness, but she seemed to be lost for words. She did smile at Lucy though, not that it was any comfort. Lucy had never been one for playing with dolls as she found them rather creepy with their fixed smiles and glassy eyes. Violet's smile was doll-like and false and Lucy didn't like it, not one bit.

"I'd better go, I think Vonk wants me," she told Violet before hurriedly jostling through the crowd, back to where Vonk and Diamond were standing, still wittering away. Diamond was laughing merrily at something Vonk had just said. Lucy tugged at his sleeve.

"What is it, Lucy?"

"I need to speak to you. In private."

"Can't it wait?"

"No."

Vonk sighed. "Sorry, Diamond. I was really enjoying our chat. But perhaps we'll have a chance to meet again later?"

"Of course, my darling! I look forward to it!"

94

Vonk, who was looking rather rosy about the cheeks, led Lucy over to his pantry and opened the door for her to step inside. It was a large room, with space for a gleaming table and chairs. All the Hall's serving dishes, plates and silverware were kept in the wooden cabinets which lined the walls. Vonk invited Lucy to sit down.

"So what's the matter?" he demanded.

"Something strange is going on," Lucy said, then explained about seeing Becky and Lord Percy together and about Violet and the boy from the alley, the trace of magic she'd seen and the conversation she'd just overheard.

Vonk was silent for a few moments before asking, "Are you sure this boy you saw was the same one who attacked you? Is there any chance one of Diamond's troupe wandered up to the east wing by mistake and that's who you saw?"

"I'd know that boy anywhere! What about the trace of magic? And who's this Valentina that Becky and Violet mentioned? I think I should go and see Lord Grave and tell him about it all."

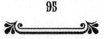

"I agree. But he's already gone out. Lord Percy is feeling much better, but somewhat down in the dumps. Lord Grave has taken him for a drive and then they're going for an early dinner, just the two of them. He said they'd be back by nine, although I wouldn't bank on it."

"Perhaps we should talk to Lady Sibyl instead, then?"

"I don't think his Lordship would like that. He's the head of MAAM: we should tell him first. Let's wait until he comes home."

✳

But by ten o'clock Lord Grave and Lord Percy still hadn't returned. Eleven o'clock came and went, and there was still no sign of them. At midnight, Lucy was sitting alone in the kitchen, hoping to hear the sound of Lord Grave's carriage any second, when Vonk came in and told her to go to bed.

"I know what Lord Grave can be like when he's out with Lord Percy, just the two of them. They get on the brandy and cigars and lose track of time. We

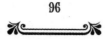

can speak to him in the morning. Mrs C and Becky are in bed. You'd best go too."

Lucy reluctantly did as she was told, determined to stay awake until Lord Grave came home. But the night was chilly and her bed was warm, so she kept almost drifting off. In the end, she decided to sneak back down to the kitchen to wait for Lord Grave. Hopefully Vonk would have gone to bed by now and wouldn't be around to tell her off for being up and about.

She tried to be quiet as she slipped out from under the covers, but the mattress springs twanged unhelpfully. Lucy held her breath, but, thankfully, the noise didn't wake Becky from her slumber. In fact, the housemaid gave a small snore. Lucy picked up the candlestick she kept next to her bed and then tiptoed out of the room. When she was safely out in the passageway, she lit her candle.

She was about to begin creeping down to the kitchen when she had a better idea. She'd go and have another look around the east wing in case the mysterious boy was there again. Even if he wasn't, she might uncover some new clues to give her something more definite to report to Lord Grave when he finally arrived home.

She began making her way down to the first floor. At the bottom of the stairs, her foot caught against something warm and furry and she nearly tripped over.

"Watch out, Luce!" Smell said, getting to his paws and arching his back. "What are you up to?"

"Looking for a boy. What are you up to?"

"Just 'aving a doze. What boy? Still a bit young for that, ain't you?"

Lucy huffed. "Don't be stupid. There's something funny going on. And I'm sure Becky's involved. Maybe Violet too." She explained to Smell what she'd witnessed.

"Why didn't you report this to 'is Lordship?"

"I'm going to, but he hasn't come home yet!"

Smell swished his tail thoughtfully, and let out a toot.

"Oh, that's disgusting!" Lucy held her nose.

"Sorry. Was thinking a bit too 'ard. Tell you what,

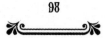

let's both 'ave a look for this kid. I don't reckon you should be doing it on your own."

"Come on, then. Try to not to think so hard, though."

When the two of them reached the corridor where the guest bedroom was, Smell suddenly stopped and twitched his ear. He gave a low growl of warning. "Someone's up ahead, can 'ear 'em talking. Sounds like Percy and Grave. Bit of an argument—"

BANG!

The explosion was so loud it rang through the whole house, making the chandeliers tinkle and the windows rattle.

CHAPTER NINE

GORMLESS GRAVE

"**G**et down!" Smell yelled.

Lucy flung herself to the floor. Chips of grey stone flew through the air. One fragment grazed her cheek, others hit a nearby mirror and vase, shattering both instantly. Shards of glass and china rained down.

"What the 'eck was that?" Smell said, shaking his head in pain. His half-ear was cut and bleeding.

"I don't know. Come on, let's find out," Lucy said, getting to her feet and dusting herself down.

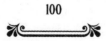

"I dunno if that's a good idea."

"That noise will have woken the whole house. Everyone'll be down here any minute, so we won't be on our own," Lucy said, and ran off along the corridor before Smell could protest further.

The origin of the exploding stone soon became clear. The statue of Lady Constance Grave was now nothing more than a pile of rubble. Lord Grave and Lord Percy, who was looking remarkably recovered from his traumatic experience, were staring at it in disbelief. The two of them didn't even notice Lucy at first. They were too busy berating each other.

"Don't talk to me like that," Lord Grave was saying. "You—"

Lord Percy dug his elbow into Lord Grave's side; he'd spotted Lucy and Smell.

"Ah," Lord Grave said. "Lucy and, um. We've had a slight incident."

"What happened?" Lucy asked, gazing at the ruins of Lady Constance Grave, which were still smoking.

Before either of their Lordships could reply,

someone suddenly pushed past Lucy. It was Becky. She positioned herself in front of the two men, her hands on her hips. "This is just stupendous, isn't it?" she said angrily.

Lord Percy and Lord Grave exchanged glances.

"We, er—" Lord Percy began.

"We don't owe servants any explanations!" Lord Grave snapped. "Know your place, Bone. Remember who I am!"

Becky opened her mouth and closed it again.

"Quite right, Grave. Do you think we should have a man meeting about this . . . incident?" Lord Percy asked.

"You mean a MAAM meeting," Lord Grave replied. "Good idea."

Lucy couldn't believe her ears. What was Lord Grave doing, mentioning MAAM in front of Becky? Had he been drinking too much after-dinner brandy?

"We should send the maids back to bed, though," Lord Percy said.

"Yes, of course. Although . . . Becky, come here a moment. I want a word with you."

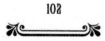

Becky stuck her bottom lip out mutinously, but did as Lord Grave said. He led her a little way off down the corridor and whispered briefly in her ear. Then the two of them rejoined the others.

"Off to bed, now, both of you!" Lord Grave commanded.

Whatever Lord Grave said to Becky had calmed her rebelliousness; she turned on her heel and strode off without complaint. Lucy was about to follow when Smell said quietly, "Don't you want Luce at the meeting?"

Lord Grave stepped backwards and stared at Smell, his mouth hanging open. "Yes, er, spot on. Of course we do. Let's get going." But he didn't get going anywhere. He stayed where he was, looking surreptitiously around. It was almost as though he didn't know where to go next.

"Are we having the meeting here?" Lucy said after a few moments, puzzled at Lord Grave's behaviour as well as his lack of action in what seemed like a rather serious situation.

"Of course not! Lead the way, Percy!"

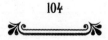

"What about the others?" Smell asked.

"Ah yes, the others," Lord Grave said. "Perhaps you could go and fetch them, Stink?" With that, Lord Percy bundled Lord Grave off down the corridor. Lucy watched them go, still utterly bewildered.

"Is Lord Grave . . . *drunk*?"

"Just what I was thinking. 'E must 'ave been at the brandy," Smell agreed. "Never seen 'im act so gormless."

"Did you hear what he said to Becky?"

"Nope. Was too quiet even for my superior 'earing. I'd better get off and round everyone up. See you at the meeting."

✳

"What on earth is going on, George?" Lady Sibyl asked.

Lord Grave didn't immediately reply. He was too busy gazing around the MAAM meeting room, as though all its contents had become newly fascinating to him. This seemed strange to Lucy, who had just taken her place at the table. Lord Grave was usually very nonchalant about all the instruments, as he had seen and no doubt used everything many times before.

"Well?" Lady Sibyl demanded, drumming her fingers on the table.

"Oh, so sorry, what did you say?" Lord Grave mumbled, still staring at the instrument cabinet.

"What is going on? Why have you called us here? What happened to the statue of Lady Constance?" Lady Sibyl persisted.

"It's obvious, I would have thought," Lord Percy replied somewhat testily, narrowing his eyes at Lady Sibyl. "Someone tried to break in to the Room of Curiosities. Lord Grave's great-grandmother usually guards the key, doesn't she?"

"Well, I didn't know that, did I?" Lady Sibyl replied.

"But why would anyone want to break into that room?" Prudence Beguildy asked.

"No idea," Lord Grave said, shrugging his shoulders.

The rest of MAAM exchanged puzzled looks.

"If you don't know, how are we supposed to?"

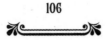

Beguildy Beguildy asked, examining his fingernails. "After all, you don't allow any of us, apart from Lord Percy, inside the dratted room. We don't know what's inside, hence we can't deduce why someone might want to break in."

"You mean none of you know how to get in?" Lord Grave asked, looking very put out at this revelation.

"George, what's wrong with you? Of course we don't," Lady Sibyl said.

"Has anything been stolen?" Lucy asked.

"They didn't get the keys, so they couldn't have got inside. I would say it's safe to assume they didn't manage to swipe anything," Lord Grave said, sounding strangely glum.

"Hang on, have you actually checked nothing's missing?" Lucy asked.

Lord Grave looked slightly bewildered.

"You *have* checked, haven't you, George?" Lady Sibyl asked.

"Hell's teeth! Of course, woman! Do you take me for a fool?" Lord Grave replied, raising his voice a little.

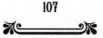

Lady Sibyl drew herself very upright in her chair. Lucy could see that she was shocked and hurt at the way Lord Grave had spoken to her. It seemed very out of character; Lord Grave was extremely fond of Lady Sibyl and she was the only person allowed to call him by his first name.

"Well, George. Perhaps if you don't require my help . . ." Lady Sibyl began, pushing back her chair. Vonk hurried over to help her.

"I'm sure we can manage without you," Lord Grave said in a horrible, sneering voice.

Lady Sibyl's mouth trembled, but she didn't reply. Instead, she turned and walked gracefully out of the MAAM meeting room, then slammed the door behind her in a most inelegant manner.

There was an awkward silence, which Prudence eventually broke. "You shouldn't have spoken to Lady Sibyl like that," she said in a slightly wavering voice.

"Oh, don't you start!" Lord Grave banged his fist on the table, making everyone jump. He eyed Prudence. Like her brother, Prudence was a keen sailor, and she was fond of clothes with a naval theme.

The purple silk dressing gown she wore was richly embroidered with white helms and anchors.

"You're very fond of the sea, I take it. Why don't you go and jump—"

"Lord Grave!" Lord Percy interjected. "I think perhaps we're all a bit kna— are all a little tired. And you're, um, overwrought at the loss of the statue of your beloved great-grandmother. A family heirloom with great sentimental value, yes?"

Lord Grave rubbed his face. "Yes. You're right. I'm sorry, Prudence. I think we should all get some sleep. Busy day tomorrow. Final preparations for the ball. In fact, Vonk, I'd like to discuss some, um, stuff with you in my room before you go back to bed."

"Very well, your Lordship, happy to discuss *stuff* if you so wish," Vonk said rather stiffly. He looked most put out at the prospect of losing even more sleep.

Lucy had been intending to mention the unusual happening with Becky, Violet and the boy from the alley. But something about Lord Grave's manner, and Lord Percy's, made her pause. Instead, she dawdled around while everyone stood up and began making

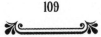

their way out of the meeting room. Lucy caught Bertie's gaze as he was about to pass by, and winked, gesturing at him to stay instead. Luckily, the rest of MAAM were too preoccupied to notice that Lucy and Bertie weren't in a hurry to leave and so the two of them were soon left alone except for Smell.

"That was very odd. And some other strange things happened yesterday afternoon," Lucy said, and brought Bertie up to date on seeing the boy from the alley. "I was going to tell Lord Grave about it, but he doesn't seem to be himself at the moment."

"Agreed," Smell replied. "Never seen Grave act like that before."

Bertie eyed them both. "Perhaps he's just tired and upset, like Lord Percy said?"

Smell licked his front paw. "Or maybe 'e's 'ad a blow to the 'ead and it's changed 'is personality? And not for the better!"

✳

Bertie, Lucy and Smell went their separate ways. Lucy wearily trudged back to bed, even though she knew she would have to get up again in an hour or two. Becky's bed was empty. Lucy wondered whether her fellow servant was up to no good somewhere else in the house. But tiredness soon overcame her and she drifted off to sleep without giving the matter any further thought. She began having a pleasant dream about Beguildy Beguildy. He was dressed in a frilly cap and apron and Lucy was the lady of the house, ordering him to do ever more unpleasant tasks such as cleaning out the chamber pots and mucking out the elephants in the wildlife park. She was just about to command that he trimmed the lawns of Grave Hall using only his teeth when she suddenly woke up.

Thunder was rumbling outside and, at first, Lucy thought the noise must have interrupted her dream. She snuggled further under the blankets and closed her eyes, hoping to get back to bossing Beguildy Beguildy about. But then she felt something tickle her cheek. She opened her eyes. A flash of lightning lit up the room. Becky was crouched next to Lucy's bed.

The scissors she clenched in her fist were aimed towards Lucy's face.

III

꙳⸻꙳

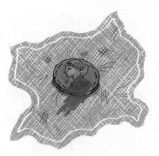

CHAPTER TEN

ROGUE ANIMATION

Lucy rolled out of Becky's reach, just as the lighting faded. She landed on the floor with a hard bump, but immediately scrambled to her feet and lurched in what she thought was the direction of the door. But the dark and the shock of the attack had confused her and she banged into something. In the next flash of lightning she realised she had stumbled into the end of Becky's bed, which was nearest the door. The room went black again, but at least Lucy now had her bearings. She was about to make a run

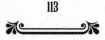

for it when Becky grabbed her from behind in a headlock. Lucy felt cold metal digging into her cheek. There was only one thing to do.

She screamed as long and as hard as she could.

Becky froze. Moments later, footsteps thundered along the passageway outside and the bedroom door crashed open just as Becky let Lucy go. There was a loud thump. The storm was right overhead now; thunder boomed above the roofs of Grave Hall and the bursts of lightning were close together, illuminating the broad form of Mrs Crawley standing in the doorway. The cook-cum-housekeeper fumbled her way over to the fireplace, where a heavy candlestick stood on the mantelpiece. She dug into the pocket of her flowery patterned dressing gown and pulled out a box of matches.

"What's wrong with Becky?" she cried when she'd lit the candle.

Lucy turned and saw that Becky was lying stretched out on the rug that covered the floorboards, apparently in a dead faint. Lucy was sure the under-housemaid was faking it, and longed to give her a kick to prove

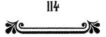

this but didn't quite dare as Mrs Crawley was now kneeling next to Becky's prone form.

"Lucy, light another candle and go to my room. There are smelling salts in my bedside drawer. Be quick now!"

With great reluctance, Lucy did as she was told. By the time she came back with the smelling salts, Becky was sitting up, blinking in the light of the candle that Mrs Crawley was holding near her face.

"Whatever happened, girls?" she asked.

"She attacked me! With scissors!" Lucy said.

"What? No!" Becky said. "You were sleepwalking and I woke you up. You were about to walk into the wall."

"Oh, Becky, you silly girl. Don't you know it's dangerous to wake a sleepwalker?" Mrs Crawley chided.

"I do now. She went mad. Started screaming. Scared me so much I passed out!"

Lucy couldn't contain her fury at Becky's barefaced lies. "That's not true! You tried to strangle me! And cut me!"

Becky looked astonished at this accusation. "I never did!"

"Girls! Shush now! We don't want to wake the whole house! Lucy, you say Becky had a pair of scissors? Where are they?"

"She must have hidden them!"

Mrs Crawley sighed. "Becky, stand up. Shake out your nightdress."

"I told you, she's lying!" Becky said furiously. But she got to her feet and shook her nightdress in an exaggerated way. It was obvious she was hiding nothing on her person.

"Both of you. Stand against that wall and don't move," Mrs Crawley ordered. She began searching the room. It didn't take long as the attic was small and there were very few places a person could conceal a weapon. Mrs Crawley found nothing. Her search complete, she carefully examined Lucy's face and neck, but there were no cuts, bruises or marks of any kind.

"I think Becky's right. You must have been dreaming," Mrs Crawley said as all the clocks in the house struck five. "No point going back to bed now, I suppose. Becky, you're off to your parents today, aren't you? How are you getting there?"

"Shanks's pony, of course," Becky said sulkily.

"You might as well get ready and go, then. If you make an early start you'll be there for breakfast. Lucy, I could do with a hand in the kitchen as soon as you're dressed. There's an awful lot to do today."

Lucy was more than happy to get away from Becky. As she made her way downstairs, the storm was moving on, giving way to a bright, clear day.

"Are you all right now?" Mrs Crawley asked, when Lucy came into the kitchen.

Lucy shrugged. "I suppose so." She couldn't help feeling resentful about Mrs Crawley believing Becky's side of the story instead of her own.

Mrs Crawley smiled. "Oh, come on, Lucy. Cheer up. Would Becky really attack you with a pair of scissors? I know she can be nasty, but even she wouldn't do something like that, I'm sure! Let's get on. First things first. Could you muck out Bathsheba and give her breakfast, please?"

Although Mr Gomel the golem had taken over many of the day-to-day duties at the wildlife park, including the nasty task of mucking out the animals, Lucy was still in charge of taking care of Bathsheba. This was because Mr Gomel had developed a taste for the raw liver that Bathsheba was so fond of and kept eating it. Naturally, this had led to some tense standoffs between golem and panther, so Lucy had resumed this particular task.

She fished out her armour from its place in the kitchen broom cupboard and began strapping it on with Mrs Crawley's help. The armour was necessary to protect Lucy from the more predatory animals when she went into the wildlife park to muck out Bathsheba's living quarters. Then she clanked across the kitchen to collect the panther's breakfast bucket. She was about to head outside when Vonk came yawning into the kitchen. His hair was dishevelled and his uniform crumpled. His waistcoat was missing a couple of buttons.

"Lucy's just off to clean out Bathsheba," Mrs Crawley told him.

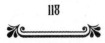

"Bathsheba? Oh, the panther. That reminds me. His Lordship says that animal is to stay in the park today. He doesn't want her at the ball either."

"But why?" Lucy asked. The panther wasn't allowed to spend her nights inside Grave Hall as she always raided the kitchen. But most of the rest of the time she was at Lord Grave's side.

"I've no idea. Ask his Lordship if you're bothered. Any chance of some breakfast, Crawley?"

Mrs Crawley folded her arms. Her beard bristled. "Any chance of a shred of politeness from you today, Vonk?"

Vonk rolled his eyes. "Some breakfast, *please*."

"That's a slight improvement, I suppose. Lucy! Why are you hanging around? It's going to be a struggle getting everything done without Violet and Becky to help. We need to get on!"

*

Once she'd finished mucking out Bathsheba's pen, Lucy made her way over to the gate that separated the wildlife park from the rest of the grounds. As

usual, Bathsheba was at her heels. Most mornings the panther would accompany Lucy back to the house and trot upstairs to Lord Grave's bedroom. But remembering what Vonk had said, Lucy made sure she slipped through the gate before Bathsheba could follow her.

"I'm really sorry," she told the panther as she locked the gate. Bathsheba growled in response, showing her fangs. "Not today, there's too much going on. Lord Grave says you're to stay here."

But Bathsheba wasn't appeased and, as Lucy turned and began trundling her wheelbarrow and its smelly contents back to the house, she could hear Bathsheba clawing the iron gates, making them rattle. She continued trudging along until she heard something else. Raised voices. Lucy stopped, took off her helmet and hung it on the handle of the wheelbarrow so she could hear more clearly. The voices were coming from the direction of the coach house. Intrigued, she set off across the grass towards it. She tried to move quietly but her armour clanked, so she had to stop a few metres away in case someone heard her approaching. She listened closely. The first voice she recognised was Lord Grave's.

"Hell's teeth! You shouldn't have even tried that without asking me, Bone! You need to realise that I'm in charge!"

"It was a good plan! If Crawley hadn't come along, we'd have Goodly and we'd know how to get in." To Lucy's amazement, this was Becky speaking. What was she doing here? She was supposed to be on her way to her parents'.

"It was a stupid idea," said Lord Percy's voice. "Goodly might not even know the new hiding place."

"Luckily for you, Bone, we got Vonk last night. He'll soon squeal, I bet," Lord Grave added.

"Shirking again?" said another voice, this time from behind Lucy. She started, making her armour rattle. It was Beguildy Beguildy.

"Sneaking around again, Beguildy?" she retorted and stalked off to retrieve her wheelbarrow, furious at the interruption. She was halfway back to the house when she almost collided with Vonk.

"Watch out, girl," he said.

Lucy stared at Vonk, taken aback at his unfriendly tone. Unperturbed, he grinned and took a puff of the very large cigar he was holding. Then he blew the smoke back out of his nose, sending whirls of white into the bright, clear air.

Lucy frowned. "You're smoking! You don't smoke!"

Vonk shrugged. "Well, um, special occasion. The ball."

"Is that one of Lord Grave's cigars?" Lucy said suspiciously.

Vonk gave a very un-Vonk-like giggle. "Might be. Might not be. Now get on with your business and let me get on with mine."

The butler walked off towards the coach house, puffing on his cigar all the way. Lucy watched him go, her mind racing. Why were so many people acting so strangely? The seed of suspicion that had lodged itself in Lucy's mind the day before began to sprout into a theory. She abandoned her wheelbarrow once again, sat down on one of the nearby stone benches and began thinking things through slowly and carefully.

Lucy remembered what Smell had said last night about Lord Grave having a blow to the head. He might have been joking, but maybe he was actually right. Lord Grave really was acting as though his personality had changed. His mean comments to Lady Sibyl and Prudence, and now his sudden abandonment of Bathsheba, weren't like him at all. Lucy knew only too well that her employer could be somewhat on the moody side at times, but he hadn't been like that since Bertie (who had been missing, presumed dead for a long time) had come home. And it wasn't just Lord Grave. Violet, Lord Percy and now Vonk seemed to be nothing like their normal selves. Could there be some sort of magic that could make you change overnight?

A sudden possibility occurred to Lucy. During the Jerome Wormwood case, she had gone into battle against the golem before it had become a more peaceable being. Lucy had defeated the golem by animating a stone angel and bringing it to life.

But she had done more than just make the angel come to life. For a short while she had *become* the

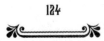

angel. She'd seen through its eyes and fought using its stone fists. What if there was even more to animation than she'd realised? Could it be possible for one human being to animate and take over another human being in the way she'd animated and taken over the stone angel?

Lucy nodded to herself, certain her theory could be true. But the next question was: why? Why would someone want to take over her friends? Could it have something to do with the Room of Curiosities? What if Vonk, along with Violet, Lord Grave and Lord Percy, was being animated by a rogue magician who wanted to gain access? And perhaps the children who'd attacked Lord Percy were working for that rogue magician?

But that still didn't explain the attack on herself and Violet. For a moment, Lucy thought she'd found a flaw in her theory. Then she remembered that *she* knew how to get into the Room of Curiosities. If Lucy herself had been the target of the attack in the alley, rather than Violet, that would tie in with everything else.

The more Lucy considered all the unsettling events of the past couple of days, the more certain she became. There was a dangerous magician out there who wanted to get inside the Room of Curiosities so badly that he or she was willing to use animation in a most dastardly way.

CHAPTER ELEVEN

LUCY TESTS HER THEORY

Excited and decidedly alarmed by her speculations, Lucy hurried off to find someone to use as a sounding board. The first person she collared was Smell. He was lurking in the kitchen as he often did, sniffing around for scraps. Luckily, Mrs Crawley was in the scullery and so didn't waylay Lucy and tell her to start another task on her very long list.

"Psst. Smell!"

Smell looked up, his mouth hanging slightly open and his eyes glazed. "Yeah?" he said vaguely.

"I need to talk to you!" Lucy beckoned him out of the kitchen and out on to the servants' staircase so they wouldn't be overheard. This staircase ran from the kitchen all the way up to the attic rooms and was used on those occasions when it would be inappropriate for Grave Hall residents or guests to see the servants going about some of their more distasteful tasks, such as emptying the chamber pots.

Smell gave his head a shake and then padded out of the kitchen after Lucy.

"Well?"

"I need to ask you about animation. Do you think it would ever be possible for a human to animate another human?"

"Not following you, Luce. Animation's usually about bringing inanimate objects to life."

"I know that! But remember what happened with me and the stone angel during the Jerome Wormwood case? I *became* the stone angel for a little while."

Smell swished his tail. "Yeah, it's true you took animation a bit further than usual."

"Exactly! So what if someone else is taking it even

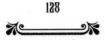

further?" She explained her thinking to Smell: that Violet, Lord Percy, Lord Grave and now Vonk were acting out of character because someone else was controlling them with the aim of getting inside the Room of Curiosities.

"Phew. That's a wild idea, Luce," Smell said when she'd finished explaining. His one eye had grown very wide and his brow whiskers were raised.

"But it would explain things, wouldn't it?"

"Hmm. Let's say it could be true. Why exactly would anyone go to all that trouble to get inside the Room of Curiosities?"

"I haven't worked that out. But wait a minute, you've been inside the Room of Curiosities. When I accidentally freed Havoc Reek?"

"Don't remember it being much of an accident, Luce. I tried to stop you, remember?"

"Yes, yes. But you know what's in there, don't you? Is there something a bad magician or an enemy of Lord Grave might particularly want?"

"Luce, I was only in there that time and one other, so I know about as much as you."

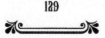

Lucy sighed, but then suddenly had a thought. "Havoc Reek was trapped in the Room of Curiosities. What if it's a sort of magicians' prison? What if there's another magician trapped in there and someone's trying to get him or her out?"

"Havoc was a one-off, I'd say. Grave only kept 'im in there 'cause 'e reckoned Reek had something to do with Bertie vanishing. Wanted 'im where 'e could keep tabs on 'im."

"Oh," Lucy said, feeling a little deflated. "Well, if it's not a person, then it has to be an object. But why's someone after it now?"

"Maybe it's the ball," Smell said thoughtfully. "It's being 'eld to celebrate old Lady Constance offing 'ester Coin. Wonder if that's got summat to do with it?"

Lucy nodded in excitement. "Good point, Smell! Maybe . . . maybe Hester Coin's supporters are plotting revenge and they need something that's inside the Room of Curiosities to carry out their plan?"

"You ain't thinking straight, Luce. All 'er original fan club'll be pushing up daisies by now."

"But what if there are relatives of hers who are still

alive? Someone who'd like to get back at Lord Grave?"

Smell licked his front paw as he pondered this idea. "Yeah, you could be on to something there, Luce."

"I need to find out more about what Hester Coin did and whether there's a connection to the Room of Curiosities. And if she has any living relatives. *And* I want to find out if people can be animated. But who's going to be able to tell me all that?"

Smell whipped his tail back and forth. "You could ask Turner and Paige, but you might not be keen?" he said slyly.

Smell was quite right. Lucy wasn't at all keen on this idea and had been avoiding thinking about it. Turner and Paige were the magical guardians of Lord Grave's library, which housed masses of magical knowledge and information. The problem was that Lucy's last meeting with the two librarians had been a little unfortunate. She'd nearly suffocated them by locking them in an airless room and then nearly blinded them by engulfing them in a cloud of Mrs Crawley's Extra Violent Mustard Mix.

These were just two of the awful mistakes she'd

made in her first few days at Grave Hall. But it had all been done with the best of intentions as at the time she'd sincerely believed that Lord Grave and the rest of MAAM had been kidnapping children to use them for deadly magical purposes. She'd been completely wrong, of course.

"It might be a bit awkward," Lucy said, sounding more determined than she felt, "but this is important. If Mrs Crawley or anyone else asks where I am, you haven't seen me."

"Want me to come with you?"

"No. You keep an eye on things here."

"Oh, ha ha," Smell said, looking offended.

"It's just an expression!"

✳

Lucy headed for the servants' staircase. She'd got about halfway up when she heard quick footsteps behind her. It was Bertie.

"Wait for me!" he said. "I've been looking for you. I need to talk to you! There's something amiss with Father. He's barely speaking to me. Told me to go

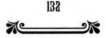

and boil my head just now. I don't know what I've done wrong." Bertie stopped to catch his breath. Lucy saw that his eyes were shining with tears, as if he was about to cry.

"He's being mean to Bathsheba too," Lucy said. "I don't think you've done anything wrong. I think he might be under some sort of spell."

"Spell? What spell?"

"We need to get to the library."

"Why?"

"I'll explain it all on the way. Come on."

Lucy set out her theory to Bertie as the two of them climbed the stairs to the servants' quarters. Bertie seemed to have grown rather a lot in the few weeks Lucy had known him and he took up quite of lot of space in her cramped bedroom when the two of them went inside.

"Lucy, why are we in here?"

"To get into the library obviously! Haven't you been in it yet?"

"Of course. It's an amazing place. But this isn't the entrance."

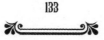

"This is the way I get in."

"Really? When I go with Father, we just go through a door. It's a hidden one and—"

"Tell me about it later. Come on, we need to kneel down here," Lucy said, indicating the fireplace.

There was some awkward shuffling around until they were both able to crouch down in front of the fireplace. The inside was covered with tiles. Those on one side of the fireplace showed a man sitting with book on his knees, and on the other they showed a man smoking a long, curved pipe.

"Turner and Paige!" Bertie gasped. "But I don't understand? How can they be on the fireplace like that?"

"Well, it's a wild guess, but I'd say that it's some kind of magic at work. Unless you can think of a rational scientific explanation?"

"So what happens now?" Bertie asked, choosing to ignore Lucy's question.

"We tell them what we want to learn about." Lucy bent closer to Turner and Paige. She took extra care to be polite in case the two librarians were holding a

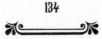

grudge against her. "We want to learn about a magician called Hester Coin, please. And about the Room of Curiosities too, if that's all right with you."

To Lucy's relief, Turner and Paige seemed to have completely forgiven her. In fact, they looked pleased to see her again, although they got a little flustered when they saw Bertie.

"Young Master Albert! How good to see you again!" Mr Turner said. "Forgive me not bowing, but it's rather tricky when in ceramic form. One might crack at the waist."

Mr Paige, who never spoke, nodded in agreement.

"Oh, that's all right, I quite understand," Bertie said.

"How very kind. You know I can see Lady Tabitha in you. Such a fine, clever woman. She was kind-hearted, too. We still miss her." Mr Turner sniffled and a ceramic tear rolled down his face, like a tiny glass marble. Lady Grave had died from scarlet fever when Bertie was very young.

Mr Paige patted Mr Turner's shoulder. When he'd recovered, Mr Turner told Bertie and Lucy to hold

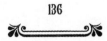

hands, which they did. Then Bertie held one of Mr Turner's hands, Mr Turner held one of Mr Paige's hands and Lucy held Mr Paige's remaining hand.

"This will feel a bit funny," Lucy warned Bertie.

"Yes, you may find it a smidge uncomfortable," Mr Turner said, which was the somewhat inadequate warning he always gave. And then it began.

CHAPTER TWELVE

A NOTE FROM BEYOND THE GRAVE

Lucy had visited the library twice before, so she wasn't alarmed when she began to feel as though her head was being squashed into her neck, her neck into her stomach and her stomach into her feet, and then she was plunged into inky darkness. She heard Bertie cry out in surprise, though.

When the squashing and squeezing was over and they were all finally back in flesh and blood form, Lucy saw that the library had undergone a rather astonishing transformation since her last visit.

Shelves lined every wall, stuffed to bursting with books.

"What are all these books doing here?" she said.

"Um, it is a *library*. What did you expect?" Bertie said.

"Oh, and I thought we were in a pie shop!" Lucy retorted. "The point that I'm trying to make is that the last time I visited here, the books were all inside Mr Paige's head."

"You're quite right, miss, for safekeeping, because there'd been attempted burglaries," said Mr Turner. "But Lord Grave feels that danger has passed for now. So most of the books have been returned to the open shelves. But we still have Mr Paige as a backup system and of course he still minds some of the more forbidden books, which his Lordship feels are too risky to be on the shelves."

"I didn't know that. Fascinating," said Bertie.

"It's one of the rarer magical skills," Mr Turner said, looking at Mr Paige with great pride.

"There is a more rational explanation," Bertie said thoughtfully. "Some people can look at something,

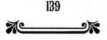

say the page of a book, and commit it to memory in a split second."

Turner and Paige exchanged glances. Lucy was sure she saw Mr Paige rolling his eyes towards the ceiling.

"Well, shall we get on with things?" said Mr Turner briskly. "You need to know about Hester Coin and about the Room of Curiosities?"

Lucy nodded.

"Let's start with the most straightforward thing. The Room of Curiosities. We can't tell you anything. Only Lord Grave and Lord Percy are able to access information about that."

Lucy felt her excitement beginning to deflate. "But this is an emergency. We think Lord Grave and Lord Percy and maybe Vonk have been taken over."

"I don't follow?"

"I think someone is controlling them by animation."

"That's not possible. Animation can't be used that way."

"Are you sure?"

"Mr Paige," said Mr Turner. "Is there any historical

140

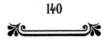

precedent for animation being misused to control another human being?"

Mr Paige closed his eyes for a few seconds, as though he was concentrating on going through the vast library he held in his mind. Then he opened his eyes again and shook his head.

Lucy sank down on to one of the nearby leather armchairs. So her theory was wrong. But now she was here, she might as well make use of the two librarians' knowledge. "What about Hester Coin? Can you tell me about her?"

"We have an excellent book on the whole Coin affair, written by Lady Constance Grave herself," Mr Turner said proudly.

"Oh, good!" Lucy said, cheering up a little. "Maybe I could take it with me to read?"

Mr Turner suddenly became very interested in his nails, inspecting them closely. "Sadly, no. I'm afraid the book is not available to the general reading public. Only Lord Grave himself can read it."

"But why?"

"I'm afraid it's not my place to question his

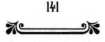

Lordship's management of his own library," Mr Turner said somewhat sniffily. Lucy began to suspect he *was* still holding a little bit of a grudge against her after all.

"What about me?" Bertie asked. "Would I be allowed to read it? I am a Grave."

"No. I'm afraid not, Master Bertie. I am very sorry to disappoint you, I really am." Mr Turner gave an apologetic bow.

While Mr Turner was talking, Mr Paige had begun rummaging around in some of the lower shelves of the library. He gave a little cry of triumph, one of the few sounds Lucy had ever heard him make, and pulled out two small pamphlets. He trotted up to Mr Turner and handed them over.

Mr Turner took the pamphlets, peered at the one on top then briefly glanced at the other, which seemed to be an exact copy of the first. "Well, I suppose you're right, Mr Paige. These were very widely distributed amongst the magical community and I expect there are many copies still in existence. His Lordship has never put any restrictions on them."

He handed one copy of the pamphlet to Lucy and

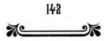

the other to Bertie. Bertie didn't bother opening his; instead he settled himself on the arm of Lucy's chair and they began to read her copy together. It was very short, just one sheet of paper folded in half to make a booklet. *Magicians Against the Abuse of Magic* was printed on the first page. Lucy opened the pamphlet.

MAGICIANS!

The redoubtable Lady Constance Grave wishes you all to be made aware of the terrible tale of Hester Coin. Mistress Coin attempted to take control of our magical world through the most nefarious and forbidden magic, which is so dreadful that it cannot be written here, lest other weak-willed magicians should try to emulate her deeds. The terrible events took place at Grave Hall on Saturday last. Lady Constance defeated Mistress Coin, who is now thankfully dead.

Lady Constance Grave is of the opinion that we as magicians need to come together to ensure magicians of Mistress Coin's ilk are identified and dealt with before they can do untold harm to both the magical and non-magical world. She therefore proposes to set up an organisation called Magicians Against the Abuse of Magic. If any magicians wish to join this organisation, please apply forthwith to Lady Constance Grave at Grave Hall.

Lucy sighed. The pamphlet didn't tell her anything she hadn't already known.

"You can take them with you to study if you wish," Mr Turner said. "As long as you return them, of course."

Lucy was keen to try to mend fences with Mr Turner, so she politely thanked him and said the pamphlets would be very useful, even though they were hardly worth the paper they were printed on.

✳

"That was such a waste of time," Lucy said, when they were back in her room. She sat on the bed and stared crossly at the useless pamphlet.

"It might not have been," Bertie replied, sitting

down beside her. His eyes were gleaming with excitement. "When Mr Turner handed me my copy of the pamphlet, Mr Paige winked at me, as though he was trying to tell me something. That's why I didn't open mine in the library."

Lucy felt a flutter of anticipation as they opened Bertie's copy of the pamphlet. It had the same text printed on it as her copy, but there was an extra page, sewn into the middle.

Dear Friend

We are a group of magicians who feel that those in positions of authority are remiss in not revealing the true extent of Hester Coin's crimes. We think they wish to suppress the information to ensure that the magical community is kept in a state of fear so that no one will question the establishment of the organisation they call Magicians Against the Abuse of Magic, which we feel is designed to interfere in the lives of decent magicians. If you

wish to learn more, there will be a meeting in London on November 10, 1750 in the crypt of St Martin-in-the-Fields.

"That's not much help," Lucy said.

"What about this at the bottom, though?" Bertie said.

Lucy peered at it. There was a handwritten note. The ink had faded to a very pale brown, but it was just about decipherable.

Meeting infiltrated by MAAM. All memories tweaked, and knowledge of the demon summoned by Hester Coin has been removed.

C.G. November 11, 1750.

CHAPTER THIRTEEN

DEMONS AND DOORS

"A demon?" Lucy said, staring at the faded handwriting. She suddenly felt cold all over.

"C.G.," Bertie said. "Constance Grave. My great-great-grandmother wrote this note! MAAM must have stopped that meeting. I don't understand the demon part, though. There's no such thing as demons or devils."

Lucy gazed thoughtfully at the note. "I'm not sure I believe in them either. But, Bertie, when Lord Grave was telling me about Hester Coin the other day, he

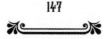

said that she'd done something really bad, something he didn't want to talk about. He looked scared. Maybe this explains why?"

Bertie stood up. "This is all ridiculous. Next you'll be telling me that seances and table-turning and all that rot are genuine. I'm going to talk to Father and ask him what's wrong; why he's acting out of character. And about Hester Coin. As I'm a Grave, I'm sure he'll tell *me* what she did."

Lucy almost snapped at Bertie; she felt rather put out that he was implying she was less important than him. But this wasn't the time to get into an argument, so she kept her annoyance to herself. "Let me come too. I could wait nearby, just in case."

"In case of what? Lucy, he's my *father*. I don't need to be afraid of him. I think maybe he's just a little anxious over the attacks and preparing for this ball and that's why he's acting strangely.'

"Well, let me come and wait for you anyway."

"There's no need, but come if you want to."

✳

When Bertie emerged from the drawing room where he'd been speaking to Lord Grave, Lucy was hovering anxiously outside.

"Everything's fine," Bertie said. He was smiling and his eyes were shining, this time with happiness instead of tears. "He apologised for being rude to me. He says that he's going to explain all about Hester Coin, but first he wants to show me something in Grave Village. He's ordered the coach to be brought round, so we'll be off shortly."

"Did you ask about the demon?"

Bertie shook his head. "I don't want to get Mr Paige into trouble for giving me that pamphlet. I'll wait and see what Father tells me about Coin and then decide what to ask from there."

"I wish I could come too!"

"So do I. But I'll report back as soon as I can!"

Bertie returned to the drawing room and Lucy hurried off outside and round to the front of the house. Despite Bertie's assurances, she still had a strong feeling that something was amiss. Luckily for her there were animal-shaped topiaries lining the gravelled drive and she ducked behind her favourite, which looked like a rhinoceros. A few moments later, Lord Grave's coach arrived at the front door. The driver went inside the house, no doubt to let Lord Grave know the coach was ready.

Lucy wondered if she should get inside the coach and hide under the seat or whether she should shortcut herself to Grave Village, wait for Bertie and Lord Grave to arrive and then follow them. Shortcutting, one of Lucy's particular talents, was a magical method of getting from place to place instantaneously, and seemed to be her best option in the current circumstances. But, before she could begin to open a shortcut, Lord Grave and Bertie came out of the house, dressed in their outdoor things. They were followed by the driver, who was looking very bemused.

"Are you sure you don't need me, sir?"

"No. I want to drive myself. Now be off with you!"

Lord Grave climbed up on to the coach and began settling himself in the driver's seat. Bertie remained standing on the gravel driveway, staring up at his father.

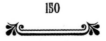

"Well, come on my . . . boy, get yourself up here beside me!"

Bertie hesitated for a few more seconds before obeying Lord Grave and joining him on top of the coach. As she watched all this from behind the rhinoceros, it suddenly occurred to Lucy that Lord Grave might not take Bertie to Grave Village at all. He could have been lying about the planned destination. If she shortcut to Grave Village and the two of them didn't turn up, she would have no way of knowing where they were.

Following them in a non-magical manner was a much better idea. Of course, she'd never be able to keep up with the coach if she went on foot, so she'd have to hitch a ride! She made a dash for the rear of the coach. She tried to move lightly and not make too much noise in case Lord Grave heard, but even so, her feet crunched on the gravel. Luckily, a loud neigh from one of the horses covered the sound.

There was a plate fixed to the back of the coach, designed for a footman to stand on, with two handles above it and to either side. Lucy grabbed these and

hauled herself up. As Bertie and Lord Grave were facing in the opposite direction and were sitting high up, she was fairly sure they wouldn't spot her.

"Gee up!" Lord Grave called, jangling the horses' reins. The coach lurched off down the driveway.

Lucy peered over her shoulder to check she hadn't been spotted. At first she thought there was no one in sight. But then something orange and furry came hurtling from round the side of the house and bounded towards the coach before leaping into the air. Smell landed neatly on Lucy's shoulder.

"Thought you could do with an escort, Luce," he said. "Don't want you getting in no trouble."

Lucy hung grimly on to the back of the carriage as it rattled and jogged down the last few metres of the long driveway. She was already beginning to regret not using a shortcut as well as not having had time to put on her cloak. This regret grew stronger when the coach emerged from the driveway and headed towards Grave Village. Last night's heavy rainfall had turned the rough dirt road to mud, which the carriage wheels churned up and sprayed all over

Lucy. Very soon, she resembled one of Busby's chocolate-covered gingerbread men. Smell managed to avoid most of the mucky deluge as he had crept underneath Lucy's jacket.

After what seemed like a very, very long time, the carriage began to slow as it approached Grave Village. It jerked to a stop to let a ragged woman and her brood of equally ragged children cross in front of it. Lucy took the opportunity to jump off. The carriage then continued for a short distance until it reached The Grave's End inn, where a groom rushed out and took the horses' reins. Lord Grave and Bertie disembarked and began to walk away.

Smell wriggled out from under Lucy's jacket and on to her shoulder. As there were lots of people milling around he was careful to make sure no one saw or heard him speaking. He put his mouth close to Lucy's ear. "Where are they off to, then?" he asked.

Lucy spat out the mud that had seeped into her mouth. "Not sure," she muttered. "Let's follow them and see."

Smell jumped down from Lucy's shoulder and

trotted at her heels as she set off after Lord Grave and Bertie. As it was a market day, the narrow road that ran through Grave Village was lined with stalls, making it hard for people to walk more than two abreast. This was actually a help to Lucy as it meant she could keep close enough to Lord Grave and Bertie to follow them but they didn't see her because of the crowds. Lucy tried to look casual as she ducked and dived through the throng, but she drew a few amused glances from the people she passed, no doubt thanks to her mud-encrusted state. There were a few annoyed glances too, as some people's clothes were smeared with mud when Lucy squeezed between them.

To her surprise, it shortly became clear that Lord Grave and Bertie were heading for the alleyway where she and Violet had been attacked. She and Smell sneaked after them. Lord Grave paused at the entrance to the alleyway and looked over his shoulder, as though to check no one was watching. Lucy swiftly spun round and pretended to be choosing a pie from a nearby stall. After a few seconds she turned back, in time to see Lord Grave and Bertie step into the alleyway.

"We gonna follow 'em?" Smell whispered. "Or we could 'ave a bite to eat first? 'Obson's 'Ot Pies are the best, you know."

Lucy's heart thumped hard at the prospect of going back into the alleyway where she and Violet had been attacked. What if the boy was there with his knife?

"Luce?" Smell said.

Lucy took a few deep breaths to steady her nerves. If they were going to follow Lord Grave and Bertie they had to do it now, otherwise they might lose track of them. "Forget your stomach for once. We're going after them now."

Lucy and Smell pushed their way through the crowds and towards the alley. Lucy tried to put all thoughts of boys with knives out of her mind. She and Smell carefully maintained their distance from Lord Grave and Bertie, and kept close to the wall where dark shadows lurked, providing useful cover.

Halfway down the alley, Lord Grave and Bertie stopped. Lord Grave dug something out of his pocket. Lucy couldn't make out what it was because the light in the alley was so dim.

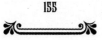

"It's a lump of chalk," whispered Smell helpfully. His eyesight was of course better than a human's.

Lord Grave began chalking on the left-hand wall of the alleyway. He drew a door-sized rectangle on the red brick, even adding a doorknob. Then he muttered some words that Lucy didn't quite catch.

Almost immediately, the chalk outline Lord Grave had drawn began to glow and pulse, filling the alleyway with an eerie green light. After a few seconds the light faded. The chalk outline had been replaced by a real door set into the alleyway wall. Bertie gingerly touched it, as though testing whether it was real or not. The door swung inwards. Bertie stepped back.

"He doesn't want to go inside," Lucy whispered.

Lord Grave spoke to Bertie and put his hand on his shoulder,

"Did you hear that?" Lucy asked Smell.

"Couldn't make it out."

Whatever Lord Grave had said must have reassured Bertie. The two of them stepped through the mysterious door.

CHAPTER FOURTEEN

LORD GRAVE NO MORE

"Quick!" Lucy said. She and Smell raced towards the door. But they weren't quite swift enough – the door was swinging closed. Lucy shoved against it, but it was made of brick and very heavy, so she failed to stop it shutting. The glowing outline remained, but was already dulling. Was there still a chance of reopening it?

"Did you hear what Lord Grave said to make it open?" she asked Smell.

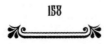

"This is where my cat nature comes in useful, Luce. My 'earing's sharper than a—"

"Hurry!" Lucy snapped. "The door's fading!" If the outline vanished, they'd never be able to get through.

Smell made a little coughing noise and began to sing in a gruff voice: "*My mask it worked, my mask it worked, I 'id myself from 'im.*"

Lucy frowned. The tune and the words Smell was singing reminded her of something, but she couldn't quite work out what. In any case, the door swung open again. The two of them stepped cautiously through it. Smell's tail took on the appearance of a bottlebrush, as cats' tails do when they are afraid or anxious. Lucy thought that if she were a cat her tail would have done the same. Her fear grew when the door closed behind them and the green glow abruptly snuffed itself out, leaving her and Smell in darkness so intense it was as though it was pressing against her eyes.

"Smell, can you see where we are?" Lucy said, trying not to panic at the thought that they might be

trapped forever in the deep dark of this unknown place.

"Just about. We're at the top of a flight of stone stairs. There's a metal 'andrail on your right. Grab that and feel your way down with your 'ind paws. Feet, I mean."

Lucy did as Smell said. The metal felt cold and rough with rust under her hand. Her knuckles brushed against the damp, slimy wall the rail was attached to. There was the slow sound of dripping water coming from somewhere nearby. Moving very warily, not wanting to trip and fall down a stone staircase, Lucy shuffled to the edge of each tread and then down to the next. At about the halfway point progress grew easier as the gloom seemed to lift a little and Lucy could dimly see the outline of the stairs below.

"We're nearly at the bottom now," said Smell. "There's light ahead."

Smell was right. At the foot of the stairs was a tunnel, with torches burning along the walls. These threw flickering light and long shadows up to where

Lucy and Smell were now standing. Voices came faintly from the far end of the passage.

"Can you hear what they're saying?" Lucy whispered.

Smell flicked his ears back and forth. "Not quite."

"We'd better move closer in, then." Lucy nervously eyed the tunnel.

"I dunno. I don't like the smell of this place. Reeks of bad magic to me. Can we get out of 'ere?"

"We can't go back now. We have to find out where Lord Grave and Bertie have gone. There's something very wrong here. They might be in terrible danger. What if there's a demon down here?"

"A demon? What do you mean?"

"I'll explain another time."

Smell swished his tail. "Let's get on with it, then."

The two of them made their way down the last few steps and then set off along the tunnel. Smell kept close to Lucy's side, his tail brushing her legs. Halfway along the passage the voices grew clearer, and three quarters of the way along Lucy was able to glimpse the room that lay beyond. What she saw astounded her.

"Look Smell, there's Lord Grave and Bertie. And Becky's with them! Why?"

"Keep yer voice down, Luce! We should stop 'ere for now. Watch and see what 'appens."

There was an untidy brown-and-white dog sitting next to Lord Grave, who was stroking its head with great affection, the way he normally stroked Bathsheba. As well as Bertie and Becky there were three other children in the room: a girl and a boy, whose matching black hair and round faces suggested they were brother and sister, and another boy. Lucy recognised him as the one who'd attacked her and Violet in the alley.

"I still don't understand, Father. Why have you brought me here? Who are these people? Why is Becky here? And what are those *things* on the wall?" Bertie was saying. The "things on the wall" were out of Lucy's line of sight, but, whatever they were, Bertie looked and sounded terrified of them.

"Dear Bertie, my beloved, dearest son," Lord

Grave said. "This will come as a terrible shock to you, but I'm not actually your father."

"What do you mean?" Bertie began backing away from Lord Grave.

"We'd all like to know that!" Smell said softly. "Summat very fishy's going on 'ere."

Bertie suddenly turned and made a run for the tunnel.

"Becky, Tobias, get him!" Lord Grave ordered.

Becky and the boy from the alley leaped on Bertie and grabbed his arms. He struggled to free himself but Becky seized him by the hair, while Tobias twisted one of his wrists behind his back. Bertie's cries of pain echoed around the cavernous room.

Lucy tensed, preparing to race into the room beyond and help him.

"Luce, no! Stay 'ere," Smell whispered.

"But they're hurting him!"

"Shh! There's more of them than us. Let's wait and see what 'appens."

"I don't understand, Father. Why are you letting them do this to me?" Bertie was asking Lord Grave.

"Shut up and watch," Lord Grave said. He removed his top hat, dropping it carelessly to the floor. Then he began pinching his forehead, at the part where the skin met his greying hair. He tugged at it and began to peel it away, pulling it downwards. Lucy's mouth went dry. Smell started growling. Bertie had stopped struggling against Becky and Tobias and was watching in shocked silence.

Lord Grave continued peeling his face off, easing the rubbery pink mass over his nose and down towards his mouth. Another face beneath began to be revealed. When the mask was finally pulled off, Lord Grave's body began to change too, becoming shorter and thinner. His clothes bubbled as though they were melting, before reforming into a purple velvet pinafore dress and white lace blouse.

Lord Grave was no more. In his place stood a tall blonde girl. Lucy recognised her at once and immediately understood why the song Smell had repeated seemed so familiar. The girl was the violinist from Grave Village.

CHAPTER FIFTEEN

THE WALL OF MASKS

Even if she'd known nothing about the magical world, Lucy would have understood that the magic the violin girl had used to transform herself into Lord Grave was something wicked and forbidden. Smell had been right. Whatever was going on here was bad, bad magic. Lucy's instincts screamed at her to turn and flee, to get as far away as she possibly could, to save herself. But she couldn't leave Bertie alone with these people. And where was the real Lord Grave?

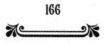

"Smell," she whispered. "What are we going to do?"

But before Smell could reply, a mouse skittered out in front of them.

"No, no. Ignore it!" Lucy whispered, fearing that some sort of mouse-related disaster was about to unfold.

But the only thing Smell ignored was Lucy's command. His cat nature came to the fore as he lunged at the mouse, claws unsheathed. The little creature evaded him, however, and ran behind Lucy. Smell whipped between Lucy's ankles and somehow the two of them got all tangled up. Lucy lost her balance and crashed to the ground. She automatically put out her right hand to save herself, but instead managed to pin Smell's tail against the damp stone floor. Smell yowled in pain.

"Someone's out there in the tunnel!" the violin girl shouted. She pelted towards Lucy and Smell, the dog at her heels. The girl threw herself on to Lucy, kneeled on her chest and pinned her arms either side of her head.

Lucy squirmed and fought. Although her opponent was older and stronger, Lucy managed to free one of her arms and weakly punched the girl in the side of the head. The girl laughed at Lucy's fruitless effort to hurt her. By now, the black-haired brother and sister had come running. They helped the violin girl haul Lucy to her feet and began dragging her along the tunnel towards the gang's lair. Determined not to go quietly, Lucy kicked and fought with every step. Meanwhile Smell and the hairy dog were having a standoff. The dog was circling Smell, snapping its jaws, but clearly reluctant to get involved with the cat's claws and teeth.

"Get away if you can," Lucy shouted over her shoulder as was dragged past.

"Not leaving you 'ere, Luce. Oi! Fido, scarper!"

The dog whined in confusion at hearing a cat talk.

"Go on, get out of it," Smell yelled.

But the dog seemed to discover more courage and launched itself at Smell, grabbing him by the scuff of the neck. Smell yowled and spat with fury.

"Don't hurt him!" Lucy yelled. She tried to dig

her heels in but she was outnumbered. She was forced along to where Bertie was being held by Becky and the boy from the alley.

"You traitor, Becky!" Lucy yelled as her captors shoved her roughly up against the wall alongside Bertie, who started yelling too.

"Where's my father? What have you done to him? I want to see him!"

"Phew. You two need to calm down, you'll give yourself conniptions," the violin girl said as the hairy dog trotted up to her and deposited a yowling, hissing Smell at her feet. "Barkis, you're not to eat the cat. At least not yet. Guard him!"

Barkis obeyed, standing over Smell, growling menacingly.

"Are we going to put 'em in with the others, Valentina?" Tobias asked the girl.

"In a minute." Valentina bent down and retrieved the mask she had dropped when transforming back into herself. Lucy shuddered at the sight of it. A rubbery version of Lord Grave's face, with holes for the eyes and a slit for the mouth. Valentina reached up and hung it on a nail on the wall alongside an array of other masks. Two were recognisable as faces Lucy knew – Violet and Lord Percy, both with the same empty eyes as the Lord Grave mask. Others were blank and featureless and some were monstrosities with eyeholes lower or higher than they should have been and grimacing mouths that flapped open.

Valentina strode up to Lucy, only stopping when the two of them were just inches apart. "Admiring my creations, Goodly? Impressive, aren't they?"

"Vile things," Lucy said.

"It's a shame we weren't able to make a mask of *you*, Goodly. Tobias and then Becky both managed to mess that up. But we might still be able to get one for my collection. Tilly, Tim, keep tight hold of her."

The black-haired siblings grasped Lucy by the upper arms. They both seemed to take great pleasure in digging their fingers painfully into her flesh. Lucy watched in horror as Valentina lifted the hem of her velvet skirt and slid a small but lethal-looking knife from her boot, along with a shiny coin the size of a penny.

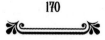

"Leave her alone!" yelled Bertie.

"You 'urt 'er and you'll be sorry!" Smell added.

Valentina dug the point of the knife into Lucy's cheek. Lucy yelled out in pain as blood began to trickle down the side of her face. Valentina calmly swiped her thumb through Lucy's blood before smearing it on the coin, which she then slipped into the mouth of one of the blank masks that hung on the wall. The coin began to fizz and smoke and the mask started to bubble and melt. A few drops of the rubbery substance dripped to the floor. Then the mask gradually shaped itself into an exact replica of Lucy's features. Lucy closed her eyes, not wanting to look at the horrific sight of her own face dangling from a nail.

"I thought you were supposed to be brave, Goodly? Don't you like your mask?" Valentina said, while the rest of the gang jeered.

Bertie began struggling again, trying to free himself from Becky and Tobias's clutches. "Where's my father?" he shouted.

"Hell's teeth, you're annoying. Right, everyone.

Bertie wants to see his daddykins. Let's reunite them. Goodly and the moggy as well."

Lucy and Bertie were pushed and prodded towards a door that was set in the middle of the wall of masks. Barkis had again grabbed Smell in his jaws. Valentina opened the door and the three prisoners were shoved unceremoniously into the dank, windowless room beyond.

"We'll be back shortly!" Valentina said, cheerfully slamming the door shut.

It took a few moments for Lucy's eyes to adjust to the gloom, which was relieved only by a few meagre stumps of candle. What she saw made her clap her hand to her mouth in horror. Smell hissed and growled.

"Oh no! Father!" Bertie gasped. He rushed over to Lord Grave, who was lying on a pile of dirty straw alongside the bodies of Violet, Lord Percy and Vonk.

CHAPTER SIXTEEN

PAWPRINTS AND FINGERPRINTS

eeling sick with helplessness, Lucy watched as Bertie knelt next to his father, groaning in despair.

"S'alright," Smell said. "No one's dead!"

"How do you know?" Bertie looked up, his face awash with tears

Smell sniffed deeply. "Death 'as a particular stink. That stink ain't 'ere."

As if to prove Smell right, Vonk stirred. He coughed and struggled to move, hampered by two pairs of iron manacles. One pair was fastened round his ankles and the other round his wrists. Lucy knew that the manacles immobilised Vonk in more ways than one: iron prevented magicians casting magic, so he wouldn't be able to use it to free himself. She ran over to help him get into a sitting position, with his back against the damp brick wall.

"Oh no," Vonk said. "They got you!"

"What have they done to you? What have they done to Father? Is he . . ."

"Don't you concern yourself, Master Bertie. He's asleep, that's all," Vonk said.

"Do you understand what's been going on? That girl, Valentina, she makes masks that turn her into someone else! She turned herself into Lord Grave!" Lucy said.

"I know, Lucy. It's bad, bad magic. They kidnapped us so that they could impersonate us."

"How did they get you all here?" Lucy asked.

"They gave us all some sort of sleeping potion. I think the blades they used when they cut us were coated with it. Once we were asleep they brought us

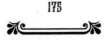

here. As far as I can work out, Violet and Lord Percy were both taken two days ago, a few hours after they were attacked. The following night the false Lord Percy went out for dinner with Lord Grave, and that's when they took him," Vonk explained.

"What about you?"

"Do you remember Lord Grave saying he wanted a word with me last night? That's when they took me. Becky's one of them, you know, a Hard Times Hall orphan. She's been lying to us all this time."

"But why won't Father wake up?" Bertie cried.

"I think the stupid children—"

"Watch your mouth, old man," Valentina said, yanking open the door and striding into the room followed by her gang. "It's Tobias's fault, if you must know. He made the sleeping potion too strong at first. Grave, Percy and that kid can't seem to sleep it off. Mind you, I'm not convinced Grave isn't shamming," Valentina kicked Lord Grave's huddled form.

"Leave him alone!" yelled Bertie. He tried to get to Valentina, but Becky and Tobias held him back.

Lord Grave moaned and twitched. Valentina

hunkered down next to him. "You'd better wake up. I've got your darling son here. Tobias has a very sharp knife, as you know. Which bit of Master Bertie should we slice off first?"

Lord Grave moaned again and half sat up. His face was a nasty grey colour and there were deep shadows under his eyes. Bits of straw clung to his moustache and his clothes were muddied and torn.

"Bertie, my boy, are you hurt?" he said in a slurred voice.

"Don't you worry about me! What have they done to you?"

"I'm fine, my boy. Fine. These young incompetents messed up their magic. I simply can't stay . . ." Lord Grave's head began to droop, like a wilting flower.

Valentina gave Lord Grave another kick. "Your daddy has something I want, *Master* Bertie. But he won't tell me how to get to it. I'm giving you one more chance, you stupid old codger. Tell me how to get in or I'll kill your son and Goodly. And Barkis will have a tasty cat supper. Makes a change from eating rats, eh, Barkis?"

With visible effort, Lord Grave lifted his head. "Very well. Take us back to Grave Hall. I'll let you into the Room of Curiosities and give you what you're looking for."

"That's a wonderful idea!" Valentina said, clapping her hands together. "At least it would be if some of the most powerful magicians in the world weren't arriving at Grave Hall right now. Do you think I'm stupid enough to walk into a trap like that? Tell me how to get in on my own."

There was a long silence. Lord Grave began to nod off again. Valentina gave him yet another vicious kick and he jerked awake once more.

"Turner and Paige. Librarians. Have the keys." Lord Grave was clearly fighting to stay awake, but whatever magic was working on him was too strong for him to resist. He lay down on the straw again and began to breathe deeply and slowly before snoring softly.

"Hell's teeth, Tobias. I still can't understand how you could make that sleeping potion so strong. Bone, do you know these librarians?" Valentina said.

"I know where the entrance to the library is, but I've never been able to get inside. Goodly knows how to."

Valentina turned to Lucy. "You can tell me how to get inside this library?"

"I could. But I won't."

"Are you sure? Barkis here is willing to take a chunk out of that cat if I say the word."

Barkis growled in a suitably menacing way and snapped his jaws inches from the scruff of Smell's neck.

"Don't you worry about me, Luce," Smell said, cowering away from the dog's teeth.

"And me and all my friends here," Valentina continued, "well, we've all got our own methods of making people who don't want to talk, talk. We don't even have to bother using magic."

Every member of Valentina's gang reached down and whipped knives out of their boots. They formed a circle round Lucy, who looked over at Lord Grave's hunched and sleeping body in despair. Suddenly, one of his eyelids opened and flickered a couple of times.

Then his head jerked a little before his eyelid shut again. He gave a loud snore. Was he *pretending* to be asleep?

"So will you get me into this library, Goodly? Otherwise we might have to start hurting your friends. Maybe we'll start with this one." Valentina went over to Violet. She crouched down next to her, pointing her knife at the sleeping scullery maid's cheek.

Lucy risked another quick glance in Lord Grave's direction. He gave a miniscule nod. There was no mistaking it this time. Now she was sure that he was faking sleep and that he *wanted* her to take Valentina to the library. Lucy knew Turner and Paige had their own mysterious magical powers. Perhaps Lord Grave thought they'd somehow be able to overpower Valentina and stop her getting inside the Room of Curiosities. At least she hoped that was the plan.

"Goodly?"

"Please, please don't hurt us!" Lucy begged Valentina. She tried her best to look terrified. It wasn't difficult. "I'll do it. I'll take you to the library!"

"We're getting somewhere at last," Valentina said. "But don't go thinking you're coming back to Grave Hall with me. Just tell me how to get inside."

"But you need me to go with you! Turner and Paige don't let just anyone in the library, you know. They'll only let me or Lord Grave in. And maybe Bertie."

"Goodly, you're forgetting something. I've got a nice Lucy mask and a nice Lord Grave mask. I can disguise myself as either of you."

Lucy's mind raced, trying to think of a way to persuade Valentina that she needed the real-life Lucy or Lord Grave to get into the library. But before she could think of anything, Bertie piped up.

"It won't work!"

Valentina frowned. "Why not?"

"F-fingerprints. Getting into the library. The entrance only works if you have the right fingerprints. Maybe you don't know. It's a new discovery, but everyone's fingerprints are different."

Lucy closed her eyes, suddenly feeling rather sick. She understood why Bertie thought this would be a

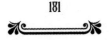

clever move, but she feared he hadn't thought it through properly.

"Just cut her finger off, then! Or Grave's!" said Tim, the boy who was holding Lucy. His sister Tilly cackled.

Bertie went pale. "No. N-no," he stammered. "I don't think that would work. The magic would know it wasn't attached to a hand."

Valentina sighed. "He could be right, we can't risk it."

"And 'course then there's me," Smell said.

"What about you?"

"Y-yes, that's what I was just going to say. As well as the fingerprint, you need Smell's pawprint," Bertie said.

"That's right!" Lucy added, grateful for Bertie and Smell's quick thinking.

Valentina narrowed her eyes. "You're trying it on, aren't you?"

"We're not!" Lucy, Smell and Bertie said together.

"Honest, it's the truth, straight up," Smell added.

Valentina thought for a moment. "I'm going to

have to give you the benefit of the doubt. Tobias, fetch a pair of manacles for Goodly."

Lucy couldn't help gasping in dismay. If she was manacled, the iron would prevent her performing magic, which hugely reduced her chances of finding a way to stop Valentina.

"Huh," Valentina said, seeing the look on Lucy's face. "You didn't think I was going to run the risk of you casting any spells, did you? I only wish we had an iron collar for the moggy."

"Oi!" Smell said. "Stop calling me that."

"Will if I want to. And be warned, if you try any feline cunning, Goodly will pay dearly." Valentina brandished her knife once more before sliding it back into her boot.

Lucy and Smell looked at each other. They'd got themselves into a deeply dangerous situation. How were they going to get out of it alive?

CHAPTER SEVENTEEN

VALENTINA'S CHITS

Lucy, Smell and Valentina (disguised once again as Lord Grave), travelled back to Grave Hall in the coach. They arrived around nine o'clock. The grounds of the Hall were lit up as bright as day; every statue, tree and shrub had been imbued with a magical icy white light, and every window of the Hall itself was ablaze with candles and lanterns.

Valentina drove the coach up to the front door, where dozens of others were already parked. If Lucy hadn't been in mortal fear for her life, she might have

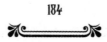

enjoyed the spectacle. It seemed as though the magicians were in competition, each vying to be the owner of the most extravagant coach. Lucy had always thought Lady Sibyl's coach with its flying horses was most impressive, but tonight it was overshadowed by a great, gleaming black carriage that had bat-like wings of its own on each side.

A couple of grooms hurried over to Lord Grave's carriage, but Valentina waved them away. She climbed down from the driver's seat and opened the coach door, which she'd locked from the outside. Because Lucy's hands were manacled behind her back, Valentina had to help her and Smell, who was tucked beneath the cloak Valentina had given Lucy to wear, down from the coach. The gash on Lucy's cheek was stinging from the gleeful scrubbing Tim and Tilly had given her face before she'd left the lair. Valentina, worried that Lucy would attract attention if she turned up to the ball covered in mud, had ordered that she be cleaned up.

"Listen to me, Goodly, and you, cat," Valentina said when Lucy had clambered to the ground and

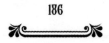

Smell had wriggled out from under her cloak. "Try anything, and your friends will be for it. I nabbed these from Lord Percy when we kidnapped him. I know how they work." She dug into her pocket and pulled out two of Lord Percy's chits. "Both of these are ready to go at my command. One's a message telling my gang to kill Grave and his cronies. You try anything and I'll send it straight away. And as an extra precaution, my gang know that if I don't send this other chit to them a few minutes after midnight, telling them that our plan has worked, they're to start hurting Grave and the others. Understood?"

Lucy nodded.

"Now, let's get inside. Keep your cloak over those manacles – if anyone sees them you'll be in trouble." Valentina turned and began striding confidently up the drive towards the stone stairs that led to the front door.

"Better just follow 'er for now, Luce," Smell said softly.

Smell was right. Lucy trailed miserably after Valentina. But a sudden thought cheered her a little. Gathered inside Grave Hall were some of the most talented magicians in the world. Surely one of them would realise that seriously bad magic was going on right under their noses?

As Valentina entered the house, the guests thronging the entrance hall surged towards her. She was soon surrounded by well-wishers, eager to greet what they thought was Lord Grave.

"Good to see you, old man!"

"Wonderful to celebrate with you!"

"Looking forward to meeting your boy. Where is he?"

Lucy's small flicker of hope that someone might realise what was going on soon died. It was obvious that none of them suspected anything untoward. Valentina's mask might be bad magic, but it was brilliant bad magic.

More and more people surged into the house. Vonk, or rather the Vonk imposter, was taking the guests' cloaks and coats. Whoever he or she really was, they clearly didn't relish being treated as a servant. Vonk's face was flushed and he was scowling as guest after guest piled him with garments.

"Where have you been?" he demanded when he spotted Valentina.

A couple of guests turned round, looking shocked. "Such insolence!" one woman said, raising a lorgnette to her eyes and peering disapprovingly at Vonk.

"Quite! How dare you!" Valentina said in a booming, very Lord Grave-ish manner.

Not-Vonk's eyes widened a little. "Yes, er, sorry, your Lordship. I didn't mean you, of course. I meant . . . the girl. I could do with some help."

"You'll have to manage without her, I'm afraid," Valentina said loudly. Then she continued in a quieter voice, "We need to get them all into the ballroom."

"Easy enough," whispered not-Vonk. "Grave hired O'Brien's Midnight Circus to do the entertainment. There's a stage set up in the ballroom. They're just waiting on his word to get started."

With Lucy in tow, Valentina began barging her way through the guests. She was rather rude about it and a few of the guests grumbled.

"What's the rush, Grave?"

"You're spilling my gin!"

When Valentina reached the stairs, she ran halfway up the first flight and then turned to face the crowd below. She clapped for silence. Lucy had to admire the girl's nerve.

"Good evening, everyone. Thank you so much for coming and I'm very sorry I was delayed. But I'm here now and the entertainment's about to start! And there'll be an extra surprise afterwards! Do get yourselves along to the ballroom where you'll be served refreshments."

A hum of excited conversation broke out as the guests began making their way to the ballroom, speculating on exactly what Lord Grave's extra surprise could possibly be.

"Hey, moggy, get back here!" Valentina suddenly called. Smell had taken the opportunity to attempt to slink off through the legs of the excited magicians. He turned and paused. Lucy shook her head, warning him not to make a run for it. Smell made his way back to the two girls, his tail drooping dejectedly.

"Sensible decision," Valentina said. "Right, Goodly. Lead the way to the library."

"George! Lucy!" Lady Sibyl came trotting towards them, a glass of champagne in her hand. Lucy suspected it wasn't her first glass; she seemed to have forgotten the unpleasant way Lord Grave (or rather Valentina) had spoken to her at last night's MAAM meeting. "I wondered where you'd got to! Where's Bertie? And dear Lord Percy?"

"They're, er, somewhere around," Valentina said vaguely.

"You're not going to go all grumpy on me again are you, George? I don't like us not being friends! Shall we watch the circus together? Such a wonderful idea to have Diamond's people perform!"

"I . . . er . . ." Valentina didn't come up with an excuse quickly enough, so Lady Sibyl linked arms with her and steered her towards the ballroom, chattering happily. Valentina turned and said in a fake cheery voice, "Lucy, cat, are you coming with us?" Then she murmured, "Remember, if either of you two try anything at all, I'll send a chit."

✳

If Lucy hadn't been in such a terrible predicament she might have enjoyed what was going on in the ballroom. Diamond O'Brien's Midnight Circus opened proceedings with a very impressive display of trapeze work, using invisible trapezes. As the artistes fearlessly flung themselves around in mid-air from unseen bar to unseen bar, the crowd ooh-ed and ah-ed delightedly.

"Oh, it's so thrilling!" trilled Lady Sibyl, waving her glass of champagne. "How can they be sure they don't miss the trapeze bar when they can't even see it?"

"Amazing," Valentina replied sourly. But Lady Sibyl didn't seem to notice her companion's ill humour.

When the trapeze act had finished, Diamond O'Brien stepped out on to the stage. "Good evening, everyone! Our next act is Madame Sawbones. We need a volunteer from the audience. Is anyone brave enough?"

Valentina grabbed Lady Sibyl's arm and raised it.

"Oh, George, you're spilling my champagne!" she said with a giggle.

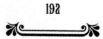

"Ah, the lovely Lady Sibyl!" Diamond O'Brien called out. "Come on up!"

"Off you go," Valentina said.

"This is very exciting," Lady Sibyl said, handing her now-empty glass to Valentina.

"Right, Goodly, take me to this library place. And quick," Valentina said once Lady Sibyl had clambered up on to the stage, and Madame Sawbones had invited her to lie down in a box and prepare to be sawn in half.

As she left the ballroom, Lucy nursed the small hope that there might be someone out in the hallway who she could appeal to for help, but it was deserted apart from not-Vonk, who was standing there with a tray of drinks.

"Everything going to plan?" he said to Valentina.

"So far. Goodly here is taking me to her room so I can get to the library and the keys."

"Want me to come with you?"

"I can handle a cat and a little girl. You keep an eye on things here. Make sure that cook stays in the kitchen, we don't want her guessing something's up."

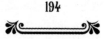

"She keeps asking where Goodly is."

"Well, think of something to say. Right, Goodly. Off we go."

Lucy had no choice but to do as Valentina wanted. She climbed the stairs and headed towards the attic with Smell at her heels and Valentina following, the buzz of the crowd below fading away. Lucy barely saw where she was going; she was too busy desperately trying to concoct a plan. It wasn't until they had reached the top of the house and were walking in tense silence to Lucy's bedroom that she had a flash of inspiration. Turner and Paige would naturally hand over the keys to the Room of Curiosities to Lord Grave (or someone they believed to be Lord Grave) without question, but they might not be so keen on giving them to a girl they'd never met before.

CHAPTER EIGHTEEN

A STRANGER IN THE LIBRARY

"So we get in through here?" Valentina hunkered down next to the fireplace in Lucy's bedroom and stared at Turner and Paige, who were of course in their frozen form on the tiles.

"Yes, but don't you think it might seem a bit strange?" Lucy said.

Valentina narrowed her eyes. "What do you mean?"

"This is the way *I* enter the library, but Lord Grave

goes in a different way. I mean, think about it. Otherwise he'd have to come up here to the servants' quarters every time he wanted to use the library. Which would be a bit inconvenient. I think the librarians might wonder why Lord Grave's using this entrance."

"Hell's teeth, Goodly! Why didn't you tell me all this before?"

"I only just thought of it."

Valentina stroked her moustache. "You, cat, do you know how Grave gets in?"

"Nah. But I reckon Lucy's right. It'll look dead suspicious to them librarians, seeing Lord Grave use this entrance. 'E's a bit of a snob really. 'E'd consider it beneath 'is dignity to be 'anging round the servants' quarters."

Valentina sat on the edge of Lucy's bed. She took off her top hat and flicked the brim thoughtfully.

Lucy frowned, as though she was deep in thought too. "Maybe . . . maybe I could pretend you're a new servant? That I'm showing you around on Lord Grave's orders? But you'd have to take off your Lord Grave disguise, of course. Be yourself."

Valentina scowled. "This had better not be a trick, Goodly."

"You've got all my friends under threat of death. I'm not going to risk their lives by trying to fool you!" Lucy surreptitiously wiped her sweating palms on the seat of her breeches. She was sure that an unfamiliar girl showing up in the library would make Turner and Paige wary. If they twigged that something was wrong, maybe they could use their particular brand of magic to trap Valentina somehow. It was a risky plan, but it might just work.

"Does this door lock?" Valentina asked.

Lucy nodded.

Valentina got off the bed and went over to the door. She turned the large key in its lock and then put it in the pocket of her pinafore dress. Then she began the horrendous task of stripping off her face. Both Smell and Lucy turned away, only looking back again when the whole ghastly process was complete and Valentina was herself again. The Lord Grave mask was now dangling from one of Lucy's bedposts. Lucy shivered with disgust.

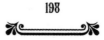

"Right, Goodly, get to it," Valentina ordered.

"Give me a chance! Come on, Smell."

"Eh, what?"

"Fingerprints and pawprints first, remember?" Lucy said.

"Oh yeah, course."

Valentina watched carefully as Lucy crouched down and pressed her right forefinger first to the tiles that showed Mr Turner and then to the tiles that showed Mr Paige. Smell did the same with his right front paw.

"Nothing's happening," Valentina said, folding her arms.

"She 'as to say the words next," Smell said.

"I want to learn more about Hester Coin," Lucy said.

The name seemed to disturb Valentina, and she gave a little gasp. "Why are you asking about her?"

"First thing that came to mind," Lucy replied.

The three of them waited. And waited. And waited some more.

"Have you tricked me, Goodly?" Valentina said, narrowing her eyes.

"No, I don't understand why it's not working!" Lucy said, genuinely perplexed.

"Oh, hell's teeth! It's your manacles, they're blocking the magic," Valentina snapped.

"You'll have to take them off me, then," Lucy said. She spoke calmly, trying not to show any excitement at the faint chink of hope this offered. Perhaps this was why Lord Grave had winked his encouragement back at the lair. He'd known she wouldn't be able to get Valentina into the library with the manacles on. With them off, she might be able to fight Valentina with attack sparks or some other magic. And maybe Turner and Paige would be able to help overpower her.

Valentina glared at Lucy, as if she could read her thoughts. "Just remember I have those chits, Goodly. One word from me, and your friends are at the mercy of my gang. Likewise if they don't hear from me after midnight."

"Not likely to forget, am I?" Lucy retorted.

Valentina scowled and fished the key out of her

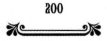

pocket. She unlocked Lucy's manacles and took them off. Lucy and Smell then repeated the charade of pressing finger and paw to the fireplace.

"I want to learn about Hester Coin," Lucy repeated. A moment later, Mr Turner and Mr Paige came to life.

"Lucy! What are you doing, bringing a stranger here?" Mr Turner said, staring at Valentina.

"I'm not a stranger, I'm a new maid. My name's Valentina," Valentina said, smiling. "I'm very honoured to meet you."

Mr Turner huffed and puffed a little. "Well, it's nice of you to say so. But Lord Grave didn't mention anything about a new maid. He always informs us about new magical staff."

"Er, yes," Lucy said, winking at Mr Turner in an attempt to signal that all was not well. "He said to apologise. He's been so busy organising the ball that he forgot."

"Is there something wrong with your eye, Miss Goodly? And what's that nasty cut on your face? Now, why ever do you need to know more about Hester Coin at this moment in time?"

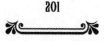

Valentina bent closer to Mr Turner, her blonde hair falling round her face rather charmingly. "Lord Grave's making a speech about the history of MAAM and defeating Hester Coin. He wants us to check a few facts. He said you were the best people to consult. But if you're busy and it's too much trouble we could see if someone else can help."

"No, no, of course we're not too busy! You are very welcome in our library. Most welcome indeed."

"Thank you!"

"We need to hold hands," Mr Turner said.

"And paws," Smell pointed out.

Mr Turner didn't look too pleased about this. "We don't normally allow cats in the library."

"Smell can stay behind, then," Lucy said hurriedly. This could be a chance for him to fetch help!

"But, Lucy," Valentina said in a concerned voice, "his Lordship said that Smell should come with us! He was quite insistent!"

Lucy glared at Valentina, but didn't dare argue.

"Well, I hope the cat's paws are clean. And no jumping up on anything. Or clawing anything. And no shedding fur. Now do prepare yourself, Miss Valentina. This might feel a smidge uncomfortable."

✳

"What a wonderful place," Valentina enthused when all the squishing and squashing was over and the five of them were standing in the library, Turner and Paige now in their full-sized human forms. "Ooh, but I've got a bit of cramp in my leg."

Valentina reached down as though to massage her calf. Lucy realised too late what she was up to and so couldn't stop her pulling the knife from her boot. Smell wriggled his bottom, preparing to leap to Lucy's defence, but, before he could launch himself, Valentina had grabbed Lucy in a headlock, jabbing the point of the knife into her neck.

"What are you doing?" cried Mr Turner. "There's no need for violence! We'll happily give you information about Hester Coin!"

"I know everything I need to know about Hester Coin, you ceramic-brained twit," Valentina snarled. "I want the key to the Room of Curiosities. Now!"

CHAPTER NINETEEN

LUCY'S BOOTS

"Don't give it to her!" Lucy yelled.

"I'll kill her, don't think I won't!"

"Oh dear, oh dear," Mr Turner said. "Mr Paige, what are we to do?"

"The key!" Valentina yelled.

Mr Paige prodded Mr Turner and nodded vigorously at him. Mr Turner ran over to one of the leather sofas and began digging down the back of it. Lucy couldn't help thinking the two librarians could

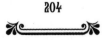

have made more of an effort at finding a hiding place for the key.

Valentina seemed to have had the same thought. "That's where you hide the key to a room full of very powerful magical objects, is it?"

"Yes. Hiding it in plain sight, as it were. Always a clever ploy." Mr Turner held out the key, which was very shiny and fancy-looking, for Valentina to take.

"You know, if it should just so happen that this key doesn't get me inside that room . . ." Valentina tightened her arm round Lucy's neck, and she began to choke. Mr Turner and Mr Paige exchanged panicked looks.

"Ah, wait. I am so sorry. I have inadvertently given you the wrong key. Mr Paige, would you mind?"

Mr Paige hurried over to one of the walls of bookshelves. He scurried up to the top of the ladder that leaned against the shelves and pulled out a hefty tome. There was something hidden behind it, which Mr Paige grabbed. Then he replaced the book and scuttled back down the ladder. He had retrieved a

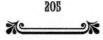

small, rusty-looking key, which he now held out to Valentina.

"Drop it in my pinafore pocket," she demanded. Mr Turner reluctantly obeyed. "Good. Now, get me out of here."

"You'll have to let me go again, first," Lucy choked out. "We all have to hold hands for the magic to work, remember?"

"Very good point, Miss Lucy," Mr Turner said.

"You're telling me that Lord Grave has to hold hands with you two freaky bookworms every time he comes and goes from his own library? I don't believe that for a second," Valentina snapped.

Mr Turner stared at Valentina. It would be obvious to anyone who had ever met Lord Grave that he wasn't the type of person to indulge in hand-holding unless it was absolutely unavoidable. Lucy prayed that Mr Turner would come up with a convincing explanation. But unfortunately the librarian's imagination seemed to fail him. "Well, it is more for safety reasons than anything else," he said feebly.

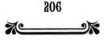

"Don't worry. I'll keep tight hold of Goodly here. We'll all be quite safe."

✳

When Valentina stepped out of the bedroom fireplace, she still had a strong, tight grip round Lucy's neck and on her knife. Smell followed the two girls. Then Valentina looked at Turner and Paige, who had shrunk back to their fireplace size and were once more ensconced in the tiles.

"Well, if you've finished with us," Mr Turner said, in a very forced casual voice, "we'll just—"

"Wait," Valentina said. She dragged Lucy over to the bed and forced her to sit down before putting the manacles back on her. Maybe it was because she was in a hurry and not concentrating, but instead of locking Lucy's hands behind her back as before, Valentina locked them in front of her. It was the tiniest of advantages, but better than nothing.

Valentina then went over to the fireplace. She dug around in her pinafore pockets and pulled out a small

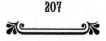

glass bottle, which she placed on the hearth. "Drink this, both of you."

"Drink it?" said Mr Turner.

"Half of it. Give the other half to your friend."

"You're going to *poison* them?" Lucy shouted.

"Oh, enough drama, Goodly. It's Tobias's sleeping potion. I want to make sure these two are out of action."

Turner and Paige looked at each other. They must have silently decided they had no choice but to obey Valentina, because Mr Turner uncorked the bottle, sniffed at the liquid inside, then put the neck of the bottle to his lips.

"No! Don't drink it!" Lucy yelled. She stumbled over to the fireplace and clumsily grabbed the heavy candlestick from the mantelpiece with her manacled hands. She swung it at Valentina, who ducked at the last moment, but lost her balance and fell backwards on to the floor. Smell took the opportunity to hurl himself at Valentina, claws and teeth bared, but she scrambled out of the way. She dashed over to the bedroom window and smashed

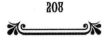

out one of the panes of glass with her elbow.

"No more!" she yelled, digging into her pocket again and pulling out one of the chits she'd shown Lucy and Smell. She held it out through the broken pane of glass. "Or I'll send this to my gang. Grave and the others will die before you can do anything about it!"

For a few moments, no one moved or spoke.

"It's too big a risk," Lucy eventually said to Smell.

"Sensible," Valentina said. "Now, you two, drink that."

Mr Turner obeyed. When he'd swallowed half the contents of the bottle, he passed it to Mr Paige, who downed the rest of it. Within thirty seconds, they were both fast asleep.

Valentina waited for a few moments, still holding the chit out of the window. Finally, she seemed satisfied that Turner and Paige weren't faking.

"See you!" She put her Lord Grave mask back on before skipping out through the bedroom door and then slamming it shut behind her.

"That's torn it!" exclaimed Smell, as they heard

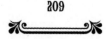

Valentina turn the key and then run off along the passageway.

"We're never going to get out of here!" Lucy said despairingly.

"If only we had summat we could use to force the door open. Don't s'pose you got a toolbox 'andy, Luce?"

Lucy gasped. "The scissors!"

"Eh?"

"Becky tried to attack me with a pair. Mrs Crawley looked for them but she couldn't find them." Lucy gazed around the small room, trying to pinpoint anything Mrs Crawley might have missed.

"The rug!" She snatched it up. Sure enough, she spotted something gleaming between the floorboards. She tugged the scissors from their hiding place and waved them triumphantly at Smell.

"But they're no good, Luce. Too thin. Them blades would snap easily!"

"We have to get out of here!" Lucy stamped her foot in frustration. Then had another idea.

"That door opens outwards because the room's

so small. I've got my winter boots on. Nice and heavy. Perfect for kicking in locks," she told Smell.

And that's exactly what she did.

✳

Lucy and Smell raced down the stairs and then towards the Room of Curiosities, although in fact Lucy stumbled rather than raced; it was hard to run with her hands manacled. When they reached the east-wing corridor, it was deserted. Everyone was downstairs, and enjoying themselves hugely, judging by the noise. Shouting to raise the alarm was useless. No one would be able to hear above the din of the celebrating magicians.

"Smell, get help!" Lucy whispered.

"Can't leave you! Too dangerous!"

"You have to! Go!"

Smell turned round and shot off. By now Valentina, once more disguised as Lord Grave, had unlocked the door to the Room of Curiosities. Lucy rushed at her, raising her hands and aiming the manacles at Valentina's head, hoping that the blow would knock her out. But Lucy was hasty and scared and only managed to graze one of Valentina's ears. Valentina swiftly shoved Lucy to one side, unbalancing her. Lucy tottered and just managed not to fall over. Meanwhile, Valentina barged inside the Room of Curiosities. She began to close the door behind her, but Lucy hurled herself at it. There was a tussle as Valentina and Lucy heaved in opposing directions.

"I haven't got time for this!" Valentina shrieked. She'd lost her usual confident manner and sounded panic-stricken. Suddenly she stopped trying to press the door closed. As Lucy was still pushing hard to open it, the abrupt lack of resistance caused her to go flying over the threshold. She landed painfully hard on the pink marble floor and it took her a few seconds to recover.

The Room of Curiosities was, as its name suggested, full of strange objects. Each stood on a plinth and was covered by a glass dome. Valentina was lifting one of these domes. Underneath was a figure made out of twigs, about ten centimetres tall. Lucy had briefly seen this figure once before. It was human-like in that it had two arms and two legs, a

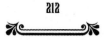

body and a head. But, as she cautiously moved closer, Lucy realised it looked much less human than she had thought. Its arms were very long, as were its fingers. Jagged spikes ran along its back. Its eyes were completely black and two miniscule black horns stuck out of its head. Its mouth was half open as if it was snarling, displaying tiny pointed teeth.

Valentina gingerly lifted the figure from its plinth and placed it in the palm of her hand. Just as she did so, all the clocks in the house started to strike midnight. Valentina began reciting:

"One hundred years have passed

Since you were summoned last

From this remnant of you

I summon you anew."

Valentina finished speaking just before the last chimes of midnight rang out. Lucy froze in horror as she finally realised what was happening. A hundred years ago, Hester Coin had broken all magical laws and called up a demon. Now Valentina was repeating that fearsome crime and a demon was once again about to be unleashed on the world.

CHAPTER TWENTY

SUMMONED

All the oil lamps on the wall sizzled and then snuffed themselves out, plunging the Room of Curiosities into darkness. The only illumination came from the stick man that Valentina still held in the palm of her hand. It pulsed with white light at first, but with each pulsation the light grew more and more orange until finally it was blood red.

The stick man must have felt as hot as it looked, because Valentina suddenly dropped it and blew on her palm. She gasped in dismay as the stick man hit

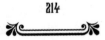

the floor and shattered. Lucy gasped too, but in triumph.

However, triumph soon turned to fear. The strewn pieces, which glowed like embers, began to move. They scuttled like fiery insects towards each other, forming a small heap. The heap smouldered and then did something that should have been impossible. It began to melt the pink marble, until there was crackling hole in the middle of the floor.

A moment later, two hands appeared, clutching the smoking sides of the hole. The hands were lizard-like, with grey scaly skin, long-fingered and ending in curved red claws.

When the demon had finished heaving itself out of the inky blackness of the opening, it clicked its fingers and all the lamps in the Room of Curiosities sputtered back into life. Fixing its black-eyed gaze on Lucy and Valentina, the demon grimaced, as though in pain. It had double rows of pointed teeth, like a shark.

"Oh yes," said the demon, stretching its leathery wings and groaning. "Just rouse me any old how.

Don't worry about what sort of *effect* it could have on me. I suppose I have to ask: which of you summoned me?"

"I'm your summoner," Valentina said in a casual voice. But in the flickering light from the lamps, Lucy could see there were tiny beads of sweat clustered on Valentina's forehead. She was obviously as petrified by the demon as Lucy was.

"Dare I ask what happened to my last summoner?"

"Dead."

"I thought as much," the demon said in a gloomy voice. "That's the trouble with humans. So fragile. How long have I been here?" The demon's black eyes glinted in the lamplight as it examined its surroundings. It had a very thorough look around. In fact, its head swivelled a full three hundred and sixty degrees, its neck crackling as it did so. Lucy began to feel rather nauseous.

"A h-hundred years," Valentina said.

Lucy expected the demon to express shock at this revelation, but it simply sighed. "No wonder I feel so *exhausted*. No chance of a proper rest. I suppose it

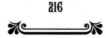

could be worse. I was captured once and imprisoned for a thousand years. And I was made to stay awake all that time. It was such a horrible bore. I really do have the *worst* luck, you know."

"Um," said Valentina.

"So I suppose I should be thankful for small mercies," the demon said. Its black-eyed gaze rested on Lucy, who smiled nervously. "Oh no. Are you the cheerful type? One of those tiresome humans who believe in finding three things to be joyous about before breaking their fast?"

Lucy swallowed. "No, I don't think so."

"Wise child." The demon fixed its stare on Valentina again. "So, summoner. Who are you, girl?"

Valentina instinctively fingered her face, as though to check her Lord Grave mask was still there.

"Yes, I can see through your disguise. What's the reason for it? There's something of Constance Grave about that moustache. Are you related?"

Valentina made a disgusted face. "No. I'm not one of *them*. I'm a Coin. My name's Valentina."

Lucy gasped. She'd been right! The person trying

to break into the Room of Curiosities *was* a relative of Hester Coin.

The demon sniggered at this revelation. "How unfortunate. There's no such thing as a lucky Coin in my experience. And your companion?"

"A nobody. She works for Lord Grave."

"So why exactly have you summoned me, dear Miss Coin? What tedious task do you have in mind?" The demon folded its scaly arms and tilted its head.

"I've read all the papers my great-grandmother wrote about you. Well, all the ones that my father didn't destroy."

"Do you understand what I can do?"

"Some of it, I think. You can kill people?"

"Certainly."

"How?"

"Your great-grandmother's papers didn't tell you that?"

"No. That part was missing. All I know is that she summoned a demon. That she wanted the power the demon could give her."

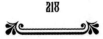

Valentina and the demon were eyeing each other intently. Lucy, who was standing slightly behind Valentina, began to slowly back away, in the direction of the door.

"And now you've summoned me. I suppose you want world domination?" The demon sighed. "I can warn you now, that sort of thing never ends well."

"No. I don't want to rule the world. But I don't want to be poor and helpless any longer, either. I want to take power and money from Lord Grave and his stuck-up friends."

"Power and money." The demon sighed again. "Humans are so predictable and dull."

Lucy was at the door now. She turned and grabbed the handle in both her manacled hands and managed to push it down. There was a faint *click*. Lucy glanced over her shoulder. Valentina hadn't noticed anything. She was too busy being needled by the demon's attitude.

"When you've been an orphan most of your life, ordered around, taken to places you don't want to

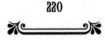

go, forced to live in poverty, you might want to have a bit of power," she snapped.

"Fair point," Lucy heard the demon reply as she slid out of the door.

Lucy hurtled along the corridor and down the stairs. In her haste, and unable to use her arms for balance, she fell down the last few steps, bashing her knee painfully when she landed. She scrambled back on to her feet and then barged into the ballroom where the party was now in full swing. People were standing around, drinking champagne, chatting and laughing. There was no sign of concern or panic – the guests were still blissfully unaware that there was a demon in the house. Smell was nowhere to be seen. Had something bad happened to him while he was trying to raise the alarm?

Lucy stood on tiptoes and craned her neck, hoping to spot one of MAAM. To her frustration, the only member she could see was Beguildy Beguildy. He was fawning over a young woman who kept glancing over her shoulder as he spoke. Lucy began elbowing her way through the mass of magicians towards him.

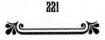

"Beguildy!" she yelled.

Beguildy turned. When he glimpsed Lucy he rolled his eyes and turned back to his companion. Unfortunately for him, she'd seized the chance to lose herself in the crowd. Lucy fought her way through the last few people standing between her and Beguildy.

"Well, thanks very much for the interruption," Beguildy snapped.

"Lord Grave's not Lord Grave and he's got a demon," Lucy blurted out.

This prompted a further bout of eye-rolling from Beguildy. "My dear Lucy, have you been at the rum punch? What's happened to your face?"

"Don't start! This is really serious! Can you get these things off me?" Lucy held out her hands so that Beguildy could see the manacles. In the same instant, the ballroom doors slammed shut with such force the chandeliers swayed. Everyone, including Lucy, turned towards the doors to see why they had closed so violently. To her frustration, she was unable to see above the heads of the crowd.

"What's happening?" she asked Beguildy.

But Beguildy didn't reply. His eyes were wide and his mouth half open. The ball-goers started to shout. Some of them screamed.

"Grave! What have you done?"

"Unlock these doors!"

"Look out! Look out! Get away from it!"

The crowd began to part, revealing Valentina, still disguised as Lord Grave. Smirking, she strode towards the stage with the demon beside her. They reached the steps at the side of the stage and began to climb them. The circus folk who were carrying away the last of the set shrank back in horror.

"Leave it all. Get off. Get off!" Diamond O'Brien yelled. "It's not safe!"

The circus folk instantly obeyed, dropping a box, which seemed to have been sawn into two, and leaped off the stage. One of them, a young man, landed awkwardly and cried out in pain. Two of his circus mates dragged him into the crowd, which surged backwards. Everyone wanted to be as far away from the stage as possible. Lucy almost lost her footing in

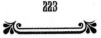

the upheaval, but Beguildy grabbed her shirt collar and pulled her upright.

"Stop pushing!" shouted someone near the ballroom door. "You're crushing us!"

"Why doesn't somebody do something?" Lucy cried in despair at the chaos erupting. The ballroom was full of powerful magicians. Surely one of them could stop Valentina and the demon?

Beguildy Beguildy looked down at Lucy. His face was ashen. "Grave has a *demon*. It could kill us all in a second."

"It's not Lord Grave, it's—ow!" Needle-like pain prickled up her back. It was Smell, scrambling up on to her shoulder.

"Where have you been? You should have warned MAAM what was happening!" Lucy cried.

"The Vonk imposter got 'old of me. Locked me in a cupboard. Only just managed to get out. Nipped in through the doors just as they were closing. Nearly lost another bit of me tail! Cripes, look at that!"

Up on the stage, the demon was capering back and forth. There were more gasps from the audience.

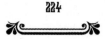

Valentina had once again begun the macabre task of peeling off her mask. The crowd cried out in fear.

"It's not Lord Grave!"

"Who is that? Is this some sort of joke?"

As before, Lord Grave melted away to be replaced by Valentina in her lace blouse and purple velvet pinafore dress.

"But she's just a girl!" someone cried.

Valentina gazed around the ballroom, smiling at the uproar and terror she was causing.

"I'm not just a girl," she said. "I'm a girl with a demon."

CHAPTER TWENTY-ONE

SWALLOWING MAGIC

"Look at you all," Valentina continued. "You're disgusting. All this drink. All this food. Lots of jolly entertainment. All to celebrate the death of a young woman."

The crowd muttered unhappily.

"I want to tell you a little tale. It's not very pretty," Valentina continued, pointing her finger at the astonished magicians. "When Lord Grave's great-grandmother oh-so-bravely killed Hester Coin, two children were left without a mother. No one in the

magical community wanted to help them, even though they hadn't done anything to hurt anyone. They were ignored by everyone. Forbidden from ever using magic."

"But what has any of that got to do with you?" said someone in the crowd.

"One of those children was my grandfather. He never got over what happened and he died when my father was just a baby. My father was ostracised too. We lived in hovel after hovel until my parents died of cholera and I was left all alone. I was only four. But I was lucky. Lord Grave stepped in to help. He took me to Hard Times Hall. I'm sure he would have put me up here in his own home –" Valentina gazed around the vast expanse of the ballroom – "but I can see space is a bit tight."

As she listened to Valentina's story, Lucy couldn't help feeling sorry for the girl. After all, Lucy knew what it was like to be very poor. And although she wasn't an orphan, her parents had been hopeless at caring for her. She'd had to look after herself and them a lot of the time and it really had been hard and

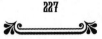

lonely. She'd often longed to have the sort of parents who would tuck you up in bed with a cup of hot milk instead of gambling all night and sleeping all day. With a sudden pang, Lucy realised that she might die tonight, and never see her parents again. Despite all their faults, she loved them dearly.

"I'm going to do to everything you did to my family, take away your homes and your money. You're all going to vanish. Then me and all the other kids at Hard Times Hall will steal all that you own for ourselves. We'll never be poor or homeless again," Valentina continued.

"You stupid child!" Beguildy Beguildy shouted. "How are you going to do that? If you kill us all, don't you think people will notice we've gone?"

Valentina grinned, picked up her Lord Grave mask and waved it. "I'm going to make one of these masks for every magician in this room. You'll all be impersonated. No one will ever realise you've disappeared."

"I don't get it," Smell said in Lucy's ear. "What does she need the demon for, then?"

"Protection? If she didn't have the demon I bet anyone in this room could overpower her. We'd stop her in a second," Lucy replied.

Up on the stage, now that she'd finished lecturing the crowd, Valentina called, "Demon! Come to me!"

The demon stopped its capering and in one bound was at Valentina's side.

"What is it, my mistress?" it said, in a booming voice that echoed around the ballroom. It clasped its scarlet-clawed hands together in a humble manner, which Lucy suspected was far from genuine, but Valentina didn't seem to think so as she glared triumphantly around. Then she whispered something into the demon's cat-like ear.

"You're sure about this?" the demon rumbled in a surprised voice.

"Just do it. You *can* do it? The papers I found said you could, that it would make you even more powerful."

"Certainly, o mistress."

The demon moved to the front of the stage, facing the horrified magicians. It raised its scaly arms. Bolts of light began to crackle between its hands. The demon grasped these bolts in its fists and threw them up to the domed ceiling. The bolts grew and multiplied until they covered the whole ceiling in a crackling net. Then they grew down the walls, like some kind of electric vine, before snaking across the polished floor. Magician after magician was struck on the feet by the slithering lightning. Each of them screamed once before slumping to the ground. It all happened so fast, and there was so much confusion and panic, that no one could get out of the way. One of the bolts hit Lucy's boots and she shrieked in agony. Burning pain ran up her body towards her head. Then everything went dark.

✳

When Lucy opened her eyes, she found she was lying on her back. Everyone else around her was still unconscious, even Smell, who was draped limply across her chest.

The lightning the demon had conjured up was still crackling and buzzing wildly around the room. Lucy

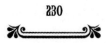

risked tilting her head slightly in the direction of the ballroom entrance. There were bodies piled up round it, as though people had been fighting to get out just before being struck down. The doors were open now, and Lucy could see the lightning spreading beyond the ballroom, out into the rest of Grave Hall. She thought of Mrs Crawley, who would be down in the kitchen. Would the lightning strike her as well? And what about the animals in the wildlife park, and Mr Gomel?

Lucy moved her head again, so that she could see what was happening up on the stage. The demon was still standing there, arms raised, hands apart. But where was Valentina? It took a few seconds for Lucy to realize that Valentina was sprawled across the stage. She was out cold, like everyone else.

The demon began to speak, its voice now so loud and booming that Lucy wanted to cover her ears, but she didn't dare move. The words it spoke were in a language Lucy didn't understand, but it sounded ancient and menacing. When the demon had finished speaking, the ballroom suddenly became completely silent. The skeins of lightning no longer crackled or buzzed. Instead, they began whipping back the way they had come, as though hundreds of electrified fishing lines were being reeled in, forming a tight ball that floated between the demon's hands. As the last of the lightning retreated into the fiery orb, the demon spoke again in its strange language. Valentina stirred and sat up.

"Is it done?" she asked.

"It is. The magical powers of everyone in this room are inside this ball."

Lucy stifled a gasp. Did this mean she was no longer magical? Her heart fluttered in panic. The thought of losing the powers she had only just discovered was hard to bear.

"May I ask what you plan to do next?" the demon continued. It was throwing the lightning ball in the air and catching it, over and over again.

"I'm going to call up all *my* magicians. All the orphans from Hard Times Hall. We're going to take everyone's houses, their money, their servants. Anyone magical in their households, I want you to strip them of their powers too."

"Only if I feel like it!"

Valentina glared at the demon. "Can you stop playing the fool with that ball? Be careful with it! Remember, I'm your summoner. You do what I say."

"The magical law is clear, I agree," the demon said in a menacing voice. "I obey the magician who summoned me."

"Exactly."

"But you're not a magician. Not any longer." The demon was still throwing the fiery ball and catching it. Each time, the ball became smaller and more compact.

"What do you mean?"

The demon smiled toothily. "You told me to take everyone's magic. That's what I did. All the magical powers of everyone in this house are now in my possession."

"But I didn't mean you should take mine too!" Valentina shrieked

The demon tutted reprovingly. "A talented young magician like you. You should know the importance of being precise in your commands. And I don't take

kindly to being shouted at. Now, I'm getting rather weary of all this. I think I may depart."

The demon threw the ball of lightning, which by now had shrunk to the size of a walnut, into the air one last time. As the ball came whizzing back down, the demon opened its mouth hideously wide and swallowed the fiery nugget of magic in one sizzling gulp.

CHAPTER TWENTY-TWO

CAUGHT IN THE NET

Valentina cowered away from the demon in terror. Lucy shuddered with fear. The demon had just consumed the magic of every single person in Grave Hall. What was it capable of now?

At first, nothing much happened. But then the demon began to change. First it became blurred as though it was standing behind a pane of particularly dirty glass, then it began to swirl into a greenish-grey mist. Was it dying?

After a few more moments, the demon had entirely dissolved. The mist that it had become began to eddy round the room. It gathered more and more speed, bouncing off the ceiling and walls, then whirled towards one of the long windows behind the stage. It smashed through the glass and vanished into the night.

Valentina was standing still, staring at the broken window. Lucy remained lying on the floor, trying to decide whether to sit up or not. Valentina might not be able to use magic to harm anyone now, but according to what the demon had said, Lucy didn't have her powers any more either. Valentina was older and stronger than Lucy, and had the advantage when it came to an actual physical fight between the two of them.

The sound of footsteps broke the silence of the ballroom. A woman ran through the doors, which had been forced open by the lightning. She stopped, transfixed by horror at the devastating scene around her. Lucy recognised her at once – she was the woman who'd helped when she and Violet had been

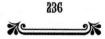

attacked, and had given Lucy a lift home in her pony and trap. For a few seconds, Lucy hesitated. She didn't know anything about this woman apart from the fact that she used to work at Grave Hall. Could she be trusted? Going with her instincts, Lucy sat up and called the woman's name. "Brenda!"

"Lucy! Stay there, chicken!" Brenda swiftly picked her way through the maze of unconscious magicians and over to Lucy. "What's happened here? Are they all dead?"

"No. Just unconscious I think," Lucy said, hoping she was right. "But they've all lost their magic. There was a demon. It took their powers!"

"Oh my goodness, this is very, very bad." Brenda began helping Lucy up. As she did so, she noticed the manacles. "But what . . . what's this? Who put these on you?"

"She did. She called the demon up too!" Lucy said, pointing at Valentina, who was still standing on the stage, pale with shock.

"Come here, girl!" Brenda ordered. Her words snapped Valentina into action. She jumped off the stage and began to stumble towards the door, clumsily weaving her way round the bodies on the ground. Brenda flung her arm back, there was a flash of light and the next second, Valentina was struggling against the silvery net that now enclosed her.

Brenda put her hands on her hips and smiled in grim satisfaction. "Netting is my special skill. Never lost a single strawberry to the birds when I was gardener here."

Lucy watched Valentina thrash about under the net. "Are you sure she can't escape?"

Brenda shook her head. "Not even if she got her magical powers back. That net is immensely strong, fireproof and completely resistant to magic. It's taken me my whole life to perfect the design."

But Brenda's satisfaction was soon replaced by consternation when the demon, still in its grey misty form, whipped past the outside of the ballroom's broken window. Grave Hall shuddered, battered by a ferocious gust of wind. The chandeliers rocked and some of the candles burning in them guttered out. Even Valentina cried out in fear.

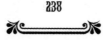

"That's the demon?" Brenda said. "This is not good at all. The girl's summoned a tempestarii. A storm demon."

"You've seen one before?" Lucy asked.

"Not in the flesh, so to speak. But my mother was a gardener, and her mother before her, and so on. I read about tempestarii in an old book of my grandmother's. They can whip up terrible weather. They're destructive enough just using their own powers. But if this one's absorbed the magic of everyone in this room, there's no telling what it might be able to do!"

"Can you stop it?"

Brenda shook her head. "I'm not magical enough for that."

"But you still have your magic! That means you resisted the demon's powers, didn't you? That must mean you're more powerful than it is!"

"I wish that was true. But you see I wasn't inside Grave Hall. I'd decided to come and see Mrs Crawley. Being here the other day made me realise how much I missed her. I was on my way up the drive when the

whole place lit up like a Christmas tree, then went dark. It was obvious something very wrong was going on. I waited a few moments to see if anything else happened and then I ran to the kitchen. Mrs Crawley was passed out like the rest of them."

"Oh no," Lucy said in despair. She'd hoped that perhaps Mrs Crawley would have escaped the demon's spell.

"We need to get these manacles off you." Brenda went over to Valentina. "Get the key out, and I'll lift the net up so you can give it to me. Don't try any tricks, girl."

Valentina folded her arms mutinously, but the stern expression on Brenda's face soon resulted in her fumbling the key from her boot.

"It won't be any good fetching Grave, he's under the influence of a sleeping potion," Valentina said as she handed the key over.

"He was just pretending to be sleeping!" Lucy retorted as Brenda unlocked the handcuffs. She rubbed at her stiff, store wrists and glared at Valentina. If only the demon hadn't stolen her magic!

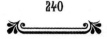

She'd give anything to fling a few red-hot attack sparks Valentina's way. Her fingers grew warm at the very thought of it.

"Oh, chicken," Brenda whispered.

Lucy looked down at her hand. Clustered at the end of her fingertips were a few attack sparks. Perplexed, she looked at Brenda. "But the demon stole everyone's magic?"

Brenda stared at her for a moment. "The manacles! Your magic was trapped inside you while you were wearing them. They stopped your magic leaving you when the demon cast its own."

"Of course!" Lucy shouted joyfully. Brenda was right. She could *feel* her magic coursing through her veins. "Now I can shortcut to where Lord Grave is and bring him back!"

"No one can shortcut to my lair unless they're part of our gang, basic protection," Valentina said sulkily, plucking at a strand of the net enclosing her.

"Doesn't matter. I can shortcut to Grave Village and then use that chalk to open the door."

"Won't work for anyone that's not—"

"Part of your gang? Well then, I'll take you with me! Or you can shortcut us yourself!"

"I think you're missing something a tiny bit important, Goodly. *I* don't have any magic, thanks to that demon! We're all finished!" Valentina yelled.

Grave Hall shuddered as another blast of wind hit. Hail began to rattle down. It blew in through the open window, clattering on to the stone flagged floor.

"We're going to have to stop the demon ourselves," Brenda said. "My magic isn't strong enough. But you, Lucy . . . Lord Grave wouldn't have made you a MAAM member if you weren't something special."

"I can't fight a demon all on my own!" Lucy said. "Valentina's right, this is the end for all of us!"

Brenda took Lucy's hand in hers as more hail bounced through the window. "Courage, Lucy. I know you can do it. I'll help you all I can."

"Ouch," Lucy said, as Brenda's fingers touched a patch of skin the iron manacles had rubbed raw.

"Oh, I'm sorry, chicken."

Lucy stared down at her sore wrists, her mind suddenly whirring. "Brenda. Valentina put those

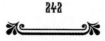

manacles on me because the iron blocked my magic. Could we manacle the demon somehow? Block its powers and the magic it swallowed?"

"That'd be impossible. It's not even in a solid form at the moment. How could we manacle mist?"

Lucy thought harder.

"I'm getting claustrophobic under this stupid net! Take it off me!" Valentina shouted.

Lucy gasped. "I think I've got an idea!" she said to Brenda. "Come with me!"

There was a terrible tearing sound as the demon's storm ripped the roof of the ballroom clean off. Rain and hail began to pelt down on to the motionless bodies of the magicians sprawled out on the floor.

"You'd better not be leaving me here on my own!" Valentina yelled. Lucy and Brenda ignored her as they ran for the door. Out in the hallway, there was a young boy lying at the entrance to the ballroom.

"What is that he's holding?" Brenda asked.

"It's a mask," Lucy said, quickly bending down

next to the boy. He had a replica of Vonk's face clutched in his hand. He must have torn it off just before he collapsed. "Valentina and her gang have been using them to impersonate people."

"I see. Or well, I don't, but you can explain it to me later," Brenda said. "Look, there's a lantern over there. That might come in useful."

Brenda was right about the lantern. Outside, all the lights that had decorated the Hall earlier that evening had been destroyed by the demon and the grounds were now in pitch darkness. The lantern, which was really more for decoration, didn't give much illumination, but it was better than nothing.

"We have to get to the stables!" Lucy yelled above the roar of the wind, which was becoming so intense she could feel it vibrating though her.

"Right," said Brenda. "Let's go!"

They started to battle against the might of the gale. They staggered along past the wildlife park, where the animals were roaring and squawking and trumpeting in fear at the wildness of the weather, as if they knew it had an unnatural cause. Although

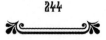

Lucy's heart ached to hear them in such terrible distress and she longed to be able to comfort them. The fact that they were all awake, alive and unaffected by the demon's spell, gave her hope that at least one part of her plan might work.

CHAPTER TWENTY-THREE

CHASING THE DEMON

When Lucy and Brenda finally reached the stables, there was one piece of luck waiting for them. The grooms, who had probably sneaked off to enjoy a few beers down at The Grave's End, had left a couple of lanterns burning. These were swaying from the beams of the stable, but thankfully hadn't gone out.

The sound of frightened horses, stamping and snorting in distress at the storm, filled the stable. Lucy and Brenda dodged their way past flailing hooves to

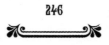

find what they were looking for – the two horses that pulled Lady Sibyl's carriage across the skies. Like the other animals, they were wide-eyed and agitated.

"I thought you said they had wings?" Brenda said.

Lucy's heart jolted. Brenda was right. The horses were indeed wingless. "Our plan's not going to work without flying horses!"

"Come on, Lucy. Calm yourself. Perhaps they're the wrong horses."

"No. They're the right ones." Lucy clutched her forehead in despair. This was terrible! But then she took a deep breath. She'd been in seemingly hopeless situations before and found a way out. The Jerome Wormwood case for example . . . Jerome Wormwood. Of course! She remembered how he'd used a special brush to transform Lady Sibyl's horses from ordinary-looking animals into winged steeds. "Brenda! There should be a brush somewhere. A little round silver brush! Oh, I hope their groom hasn't taken it with him!"

"What about that?" Brenda said, pointing to a

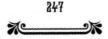

leather bag hanging from a hook on the wall of the stable. Lucy grabbed it and rummaged through it. She pulled out a few apples and a currycomb, and then spotted the brush she was looking for, nestled at the bottom.

Lucy took the brush and began to gently run it along the side of one of the horses. The brush glowed as she worked. Sparks danced along the horse's skin and its wings began to unfold.

"How beautiful," Brenda said softly.

"I know." Lucy carried on brushing until the horse's wings were fully unfurled. Then she moved on to its mane and tail, grooming them until they were fluffy and whisper-light.

Lucy repeated the process with the other horse. As she worked, she found that the grooming had a soothing effect on the two animals. They became calmer and steadier, even though the storm raged on outside.

"I think we're ready," Lucy said when both the horses were fully transformed. Her voice was slightly unsteady.

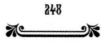

"Right you are," Brenda said in an impressively matter-of-fact manner. "Time to chase a demon, chicken!"

*

Because the flying horses looked so ethereal and their wings so delicate, Lucy was worried that they might not be able to stay aloft in the powerful storm the demon had raised. But the horses were more resilient than they appeared. Although the gales buffeted them up and down, they were strong enough to keep flying.

Lucy and Brenda had also been lucky and had found some wet-weather gear in the stable, including hooded cloaks made out of a rubbery material that reminded Lucy uncomfortably of Valentina's masks.

When they'd flown high enough, the two of them reined in the horses. An enormous bolt of lightning lit up the sky and for a few seconds the grey mass that was the demon could be seen whirling around the spire of St Isan's, the church in Grave Village.

"We need to head for the church," Lucy yelled to

Brenda, pointing at the spire. Lucy's horse neighed and galloped off immediately, as did Brenda's.

Neither of them had been expecting this. Brenda screamed and grabbed at her horse's mane. Lucy herself began to topple sideways and for a dizzying, terrifying moment thought she was about to fall to her death. She squeezed her legs tightly into her horse's sides and managed to right herself.

"They must understand what we say!" bellowed Brenda as the horses charged onwards. Lucy would have found this hard to believe if it hadn't been for her recent experience with the window-cleaning giraffe.

As they reached the church spire, the grey mist started to change. It formed into the shape of a face, with flickering lightning for eyes and mouth.

"Lucy Goodly!" the face boomed.

Lucy and Brenda both told their horses to stop at once. Neither of them wanted to get any closer to the demon. Its mouth was so huge it could have swallowed the horses and riders in one easy gulp.

Although Lucy's horse was steadfastly hovering

in the air, Lucy could feel it trembling. She patted its neck, to soothe her own terror as much as the horse's.

"Yes, that's me!" Lucy shouted, wondering how the demon knew her name.

"Why have you followed me?"

"I-I wanted to talk to you."

The demon heaved a sigh, sending a squall of wind rushing towards the high street of Grave Village. There was a loud creak, followed by an even louder crash as a tree was uprooted and fell over, blocking the road. "What is it?"

Lucy turned her face away from the demon. "I can't talk to you like this," she said, trying to play for time. "You're too scary."

The demon laughed. "I am rather impressive, I know. But I understand. I can take any form you like, Lucy Goodly."

"How do you know my name?" Lucy shouted, her face still turned away from the demon.

"I took all the magic and knowledge from those puny magicians. Everything they know, I know.

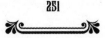

Anyway, let's get this over with so I can continue with my wanton destruction."

"Will you take a form that won't scare me first, then? Can I choose?"

"Yes, yes. As I'm probably going to kill you and that old woman over there very shortly, I'll let you have that privilege."

"I'm not old!" Brenda said indignantly.

"Caruthers! Take the form of Caruthers!" yelled Lucy.

The demon's fiery eyes slitted as it considered this strange request. "Caruthers?"

"If you have all the . . . *knowledge from those puny magicians*, you'll know who Caruthers is. Or are you just making empty boasts?"

"I could snuff you out in a second, Lucy. Empty boasts! Watch this!"

Lucy turned back to face the demon, exchanging a quick glance with Brenda, who nodded encouragement. The demon began to dissolve into a whirling mist once more. A few seconds later it started to reform into a frog-like shape, until a giant-sized

version of Caruthers, Violet's beloved woollen toy, was bobbing alongside the spire.

Lucy snorted quietly. The idea of asking the demon to take the form of Caruthers had come to her from nowhere, but it was a good notion, because the demon's appearance was now so comical it seemed less frightening. But she knew it could still kill her instantly if it wanted to. What she had to do now was keep it talking.

"I want to join forces with you," Lucy said. "You see, I'm extra powerful. The most powerful magician of my time, I reckon."

"That's a very presumptuous claim."

"Well, even you couldn't take my magic along with everyone else's, could you?" Lucy flicked her gaze towards Brenda, who had her arm behind her head as though she was about to throw something, and then back to the demon.

"That's very true. Can you explain why?" The demon still had its button eyes fixed on Lucy.

"I'm not sure I want to," Lucy said. "I don't trust you yet. You see—"

There was sharp whistle as the net that Brenda had conjured up whipped through the air towards the demon. Brenda's aim was true, and for one heart-jolting moment it seemed as though Lucy's plan was going to work. But at the very last second, a blast of wind blew the net off course and it began coiling away from its target. As it started to fall, a single silvery strand caught on one of the demon's button eyes, which immediately began to melt and smoke. The demon roared in agony. It flailed its arms, sending a jet of flame shooting towards Lucy and Brenda. The jet missed its mark, but the cuff of Brenda's right sleeve blazed. Brenda screamed, beating at the flames with her gloved left hand. Lucy flew towards her to help.

"No, I'm all right! Get that net!"

Lucy dug her heels into her horse's flanks, urging it towards the monstrous frog. If she could grab the net, she might still be able to throw it back over the demon. But the demon was already freeing itself in the most horrific manner imaginable. It ripped off the button eye the net was caught on. Lucy lunged to seize the net as it fell. But it was no good. The demon sent a squall of wind whipping towards the net, sending it twirling away. Lucy watched it float off, fear squeezing all the breath from her lungs.

CHAPTER TWENTY-FOUR

CARUTHERS ATTACKS

Now that it had lost an eye, the demon no longer looked ridiculous and unthreatening in its knitted frog form. A jagged hole blazed where the button had been, reminding Lucy of the fiery pit the demon had emerged from, back in the Room of Curiosities.

"Can you make another net?" Lucy yelled to Brenda.

"No, I can't move my hand, too painful," Brenda shouted back, her face grim.

"Can't you make one with your left hand?"

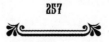

Brenda shook her head. "My right hand's my net-making hand. What are we going to do?"

In desperation, Lucy swiftly flung a flurry of attack sparks at the demon, and they hit its remaining button eye. The demon roared with rage. It pointed one of its webbed front feet at Brenda and Lucy and sent another bolt of lightning hurtling towards them. Lucy's horse swerved out of the way, just in time. But Brenda's horse reacted too slowly. The lightning struck it square in the chest. The horse neighed once, and then rolled over on to its back. Brenda was unseated but managed to keep hold of the horse's mane as the two of them overturned. She dangled there, hundreds of feet above the ground.

"Get underneath her!" Lucy yelled to her own horse, urging it towards its stricken companion. The horse obeyed, positioning itself underneath the terrified woman. Brenda's horse was barely alive now, its wings moving just enough to keep it in the air.

"Brenda, let go of the mane! I'll catch you!" Lucy yelled.

Brenda looked down at Lucy, her eyes wide with fear. "I can't! I'll fall to my death!"

"You definitely will if you don't let go!" The dying horse's wings were flapping more and more slowly. When they stopped beating completely, it would plummet from the sky, taking Brenda with it!

Brenda squeezed her eyes shut and released her grasp on the horse's mane. She screamed as she plunged towards Lucy, who tried to grab her, but failed. Luckily Lucy's horse managed to catch Brenda by the collar using its teeth. Above them, Brenda's horse's wings gave a final weak flutter and then it fell. Lucy's horse dodged out of the path of its plummeting comrade. Lucy watched, horror-struck at the fate of the beautiful creature, but she shoved her feelings deep down inside herself. She couldn't afford to think about it now, not while there was a demon on the loose.

"We need to get back down to earth!" Brenda shouted from her precarious position, dangling from the horse's jaws. The horse understood Brenda's command and began to gallop towards to the ground. It moved so fast that the wind whistled in Lucy's ears. The demon pursued them, whipping up the wind again

and shooting bolts of lightning. Lucy turned and hurled spark after spark at the giant creature, aiming each time for its button eye, hoping to somehow damage the demon's eyesight and spoil its aim.

But the demon's vision remained sharp enough for it to fling yet another flash of lightning. Again, the horse dodged away, but not quite quickly enough. The bolt grazed Lucy's knee, burning a hole in her trousers and scorching her skin. Lucy screamed and almost lost her balance. It was no good – the demon was going to kill all three of them!

"Look, chicken!" Brenda yelled, pointing downwards.

Lucy's heart lurched. There was some kind of bizarre monster flying in their direction. Had it been called up by the demon? But fear soon turned to relief when she saw it was in fact four of the pelicans from the wildlife park, looking much larger than normal. Each of them held a corner of Brenda's net in its beak and, to Lucy's delight, Lord Grave was riding on the back of one of them.

"You escaped! How?" she yelled.

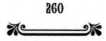

"No time to explain, Lucy!" Lord Grave sent an enormous mass of attack sparks at the demon, hitting it between its mismatched eyes and setting its forehead alight. Lucy followed Lord Grave's example and released another volley of her own. She yelled in triumph as they hit the very centre of the demon's remaining button eye, which began to melt. The demon uttered a high-pitched shriek as the flames burning its forehead away spread to the rest of its head. With the enemy safely incapacitated, Lord Grave and the pelicans flew higher until they were hovering above the demon. They released the net, which dropped neatly over the demon, enveloping it.

"Lucy, we need to seal the bottom of the net!" Lord Grave yelled.

He commanded his pelican towards the demon's feet. Lucy swiftly followed. She and Lord Grave worked their way along the edges of the net, Lucy holding it closed, while Lord Grave sealed the join with attack sparks. These were hot enough to melt the silver and fuse it together so that the demon was unable to escape. The other three pelicans then grabbed the net in their beaks.

"Are you all right, Brenda?" Lord Grave called.

"Feel a bit woozy. It's the pain," Brenda replied. Her face was dripping with sweat.

"We're going back to Grave Hall. This is almost over," Lord Grave said reassuringly.

He was right. It *was* almost over. Trapped inside the net, unable to break out of the silver prison it created, the demon continued writhing as its Caruthers form burned away. It smoked and crackled, leaving behind the small, immobile stick-like figure that Valentina had brought to life in the Room of Curiosities only a couple of hours earlier. Although it very much seemed like a lifetime ago to Lucy.

*

When Lord Grave, Lucy and Brenda touched down on Grave Hall's gravel drive, Bertie and Mrs Crawley were waiting for them outside the front door. Bertie helped Lord Grave dismount from his pelican. Mrs Crawley crouched next to Brenda, who was sitting

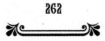

dazedly where the flying horse had gently deposited her.

"Brenda! What are you doing here? Your hand!"

"It's a long story, Bernie," said Brenda. "But I need your help. I don't think I can get up on my own."

"Take Brenda inside, Mrs Crawley. Find her a room," Lord Grave said.

"Are you sure?" Brenda asked. "You told me never to darken the doors of the Hall again."

Lord Grave coughed. "Brenda. I owe you an apology. I should never have tried to interfere with your choice of tomato feed."

Lucy frowned. "You two fell out over tomato feed? I thought it was something serious!"

"I do think I'd like to have a lie-down now," Brenda said hurriedly, looking rather shamefaced.

"You do that. We can talk more later," Lord Grave said. He picked up the net containing the demon and slung it over his shoulder before climbing the steps to the front door. Lucy and Bertie followed him.

"How did you manage to escape?" Lucy asked Lord Grave as they headed towards the ballroom.

"Becky and the others went outside to see what was happening. They were all very jumpy because Valentina hadn't been in contact."

"She had some of Lord Percy's chits. She was supposed to send one to the gang just after midnight to say the plans had worked," Lucy told him.

"Ah. That explains why they panicked when they saw the demon hovering above the church. They thought Valentina must be dead. While they were all arguing about what to do next, I persuaded Becky to free us. I promised that if she did, I would forgive the part she's played in this debacle. Bertie carried Violet out of the lair, Vonk and I carried Lord Percy. Once we were in Grave Village I was able to shortcut us back to Grave Hall."

"Are Violet and Lord Percy all right?" Lucy asked.

"Still a little sleepy. They're both in bed," Lord Grave replied, striding to the ballroom entrance. Prone magicians were strewn across the floor, just as they had been when Lucy and Brenda left to go after the demon.

"Are they going to stay like that, Father?" Bertie asked.

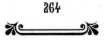

"I can't be certain, but I have a hunch that once the demon is back in the Room of Curiosities and safely imprisoned again, the magic it absorbed will be returned to its rightful owners. But we won't know until we try."

The three of them climbed the stairs to the first floor and the Room of Curiosities. Lucy was relieved to see that the fiery hole the demon had climbed out of was now no more than a very large burn on the pink marble.

"Mrs Crawley won't be pleased about this floor. Demonic scorch marks are impossible to remove," Lord Grave remarked as he placed the demon on the plinth Valentina had taken it from.

"Why don't you take the net off?" Bertie asked.

"I think a little extra protection wouldn't go amiss," Lord Grave replied, wrapping Brenda's net tightly round the demon. Then he picked up the glass dome and began lowering it carefully over the unnatural creature. As he did so, skeins of lightening popped and crackled around the demon's stick-like form, gathering themselves into a small ball that zoomed out from under the dome with a sharp whistling noise.

"What's happening?" Lucy asked, fearful that the demon might be coming to life again.

"I'm not entirely sure, but I think the demon's magic is reversing," Lord Grave said as he finished placing the dome over the demon. The fiery ball began bouncing off the walls. Lord Grave watched it intently for a few seconds.

"I think it wants to get out," he said and opened the door. The ball whizzed out of the Room of Curiosities at top speed, and headed towards the stairs.

"Come on, let's follow it!" Lord Grave said.

The three of them hurried out of the room, Lord Grave pausing to lock the door behind them. As they sprinted for the stairs, there was a blindingly bright flash.

❋

Downstairs, a crowd of newly awake, dazed and extremely confused magicians were surging from the ballroom into the hallway and scrambling to get

outside. Lady Sibyl was among them. When she spotted Lucy and the others coming down the stairs, she pushed her way through the crowd towards them. The peacock feathers in her hair, now singed and very sorry-looking, fluttered as she went. She flung her arms round Lord Grave's neck.

"George! We thought you were . . ." she exclaimed, before bursting into tears.

"I very nearly was, along with everyone else. Lucy's quick thinking saved us all," Lord Grave said, awkwardly patting Lady Sibyl's back.

"I couldn't have done it without your flying horses, Lady Sibyl," Lucy said and then paused. "The demon killed one of them. I'm so sorry."

Lady Sibyl unhooked her arms from Lord Grave's neck and stared at Lucy.

"The other horse is safe. It's just outside, Sibyl," Lord Grave said gently. "I'll take you to it."

And although Lucy had always thought Lord Grave wasn't the hand-holding type, that didn't stop him taking Lady Sibyl's. Lucy and Bertie followed as Lord Grave steered her through the throng of bewildered magicians, some of whom tried to accost him.

"Grave! There you are! What on earth's been happening?"

"Where are you going now?"

"All in good time," Lord Grave replied calmly, continuing on his way.

The surviving flying horse was still standing near the front door, where Lucy had left it when she dismounted. It neighed pitifully when it saw Lady Sibyl. Lucy was sure she saw a tear trickle from the animal's eye, and her own eyes grew wet as Lady Sibyl patted the horse's neck and said, "Oh, my lovely Rory, what will we do without Peggy?"

While Lady Sibyl continued to comfort the grieving horse, the crowd surging out of Grave Hall began yelling angrily.

"There she is!"

"Get the little villain!"

"She could have killed us all!"

Valentina had somehow managed to escape from Brenda's net, perhaps aided by the reversal of magic

which had occurred when Lord Grave imprisoned the demon once more, and was trying to make a run for it. The magicians, who had nearly lost their magic for good, and might have lost their lives too, were grabbing at her as she tried to flee.

"Stop!" Lucy shouted. "Stop hurting her! Lord Grave, do something!"

Lord Grave shoved his way into the crowd and grabbed Valentina, pulling her to safety.

"Listen, everyone!" he shouted. "Listen to me! Yes, the girl did wrong. But I think *we* may have wronged *her*. She and the other children who escaped Hard Times Hall must have been very unhappy there. We need to find out why before we condemn her. If you'd all like to go back inside, you can retire to your bedrooms if you wish and get some sleep. My servants will provide anything you need. Or feel free to go back to your own homes if you prefer."

"What about the demon?" someone shouted.

"The demon can't harm you, it's powerless now. We're all safe. We all still have our magic. We've a lot to be thankful for."

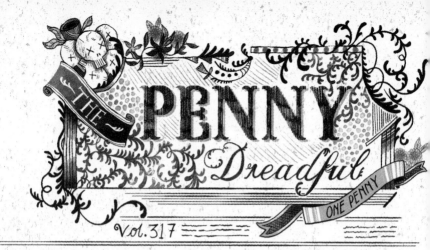

THE PENNY Dreadful

THE — ONE PENNY

Vol. 317

HOT PIE SCANDAL HITS LORD GRAVE'S ORPHANAGE!

IN A SINISTER turn of events, Lord Grave has shut down Hard Times Hall. He has refused to say why he has taken this action and where the orphan children have been taken. Our intrepid reporter Slimeous Osburn has investigated and concluded that Lord Grave is in cahoots with the infamous makers of Hobson's Hot Pies. The *Penny* has long had suspicions about the ingredients used by Hobson. However, Sir Absalom Balderdash, who has recently returned

from a working holiday examining fossilised zombie droppings, is of the opinion that the children were taken by the flesh-eating zombies he has persistently warned about. The *Penny* is unsure which of these theories is correct, so in the meantime advises its loyal readers to avoid Hobson's Hot Pies until further notice and also to take precautions against zombie attack. Sir Absalom's *Guide to Surviving the Zombie Apocalypse in Seven Easy Stages* is enclosed as a special pull-out-and-keep supplement.

CHAPTER TWENTY-FIVE

THE END OF HARD TIMES HALL

few flakes of early November snow drifted down
as Lady Sibyl lifted a large pair of scissors and
cut through the blue ribbon draped across the
chest of the winged horse standing proudly in
front of her. Lord Grave, Bertie, Lucy and the other
magical servants who were gathered round clapped as
the ribbon fell to the ground.

"It really is beautiful, and a wonderful tribute,"
Lady Sibyl said, stepping back to admire not a real
horse, but the topiary created by Brenda in memory

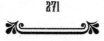

of Peggy, who had died during the battle with the demon.

"Thank you, Lady Sibyl," Brenda said.

After the recent terrible events, Lord Grave and Brenda had settled their differences. Brenda was back doing her old gardening job and living at Grave Hall once again, much to Lucy and Mrs Crawley's delight.

Lord Grave rubbed his hands together. "It's a little chilly out here, let's all get inside and warm ourselves at the drawing-room fire!"

"Sounds like a good idea to me, Grave," Smell said.

"I'll bring up the cocoa jug," Mrs Crawley said. "I made a vat of my special recipe in honour of the unveiling of Peggy's topiary." She hurried off round the back of the house.

"Oh dear," Lord Grave said when Mrs Crawley was out of sight.

"I fear we're in for an experimental cocoa horror of some description," Vonk added.

"Don't worry," Brenda said. "I happen to know that someone swapped Bernie's special spider syrup for a more traditional vanilla flavour."

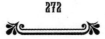

"You'd better be right," Becky said. "I'm not drinking anything with spiders' legs in it!" She turned and strode back to the house.

"You'd think she'd be grateful," Lucy said to Brenda as they watched Becky stamping up the steps to the front door. "Lord Grave could have sacked her for what she did. Or had her put in prison."

"Some people are never happy, however much good fortune comes their way, chicken. Come on, let's get out of the cold. It's more like December than November out here!"

As she followed Brenda back to the house, Lucy thought about the good fortune that had come Becky's way, and the way of all of the other orphans from Hard Times Hall. Once the demon had been safely returned to the Room of Curiosities, Lord Grave had called a meeting of all the magicians who had been at the ball. After much discussion and argument it had been decided that Hard Times Hall would be closed and the orphans offered homes with willing magicians.

"It's the right thing to do," Lord Grave had said.

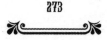

"Children deserve to have families, I see that now. If we had all given a little more thought to how we cared for these orphans, the demon might never have been summoned."

And so all of Valentina's gang had been found homes. Valentina (and Barkis) had gone to live with Lady Sibyl, and Tobias with Lord Percy. Mrs Crawley's cousin, the owner of Surprising Supplies, had volunteered to adopt Tim and Tilly, and Beguildy and Prudence Beguildy had taken on the boy who'd impersonated Vonk. The rest of the Hard Times Hall orphans were adopted by various other magicians. As for Becky, she had resolutely said she wanted to stay where she was and continue working as a maid at Grave Hall. This had naturally surprised everyone, but Lucy suspected that deep down Becky was fond of Vonk and Mrs Crawley, and maybe even Violet, and saw them as her family.

Lord Grave's drawing room was warm and cosy after the chill of the November afternoon. A fire burned brightly in the grate, and Bathsheba was stretched out on the hearth rug. Mrs Crawley soon arrived with the cocoa jug and to everyone's relief there were no spider body-parts to be found floating in their drinks.

When the cocoa was finished, the servants went back down to the kitchen, but Lord Grave asked Lucy to stay behind with him, Bertie, Lady Sibyl and Smell. Lady Sibyl kept beaming at Lucy. Bertie was grinning too. Even Smell looked as though he was happy about something. Being a cat, he couldn't smile, but he kept slowly blinking his eye at Lucy in an affectionate sort of way.

"Come with me," Lord Grave told Lucy, beckoning her out of the drawing room. As she followed him into the hallway and then upstairs to the first floor, Lucy grew more and more nervous, worried that she'd done something wrong. Lord Grave strode off down the east-wing corridor, past the statue of his great-grandmother, which had been magically restored, past the Room of Curiosities and round the corner to the bedrooms that Lucy had searched when she'd gone looking for Violet a few weeks before. Lord Grave opened the door

to one of these and waved Lucy inside. Bertie and Lady Sibyl followed her, with Smell trotting at their heels.

It was a beautiful room. The bed was hung with heavy red curtains. Floor-to-ceiling windows looked out over the grounds of the Hall and the wildlife park. Thick rugs stopped the draughts blowing up between the floorboards. A fire had been lit in the large fireplace, and crackled in a most inviting way.

Lord Grave coughed and said, "Welcome to your new room, Lucy."

Lucy stared at him. "This is for *me*?"

"Yes!" Bertie said, his voice high with excitement. "You're living with us now, as a proper member of the Grave family! You don't have to share that poky little bedroom with Becky any longer!"

"Congratulations," Lady Sibyl said. She bent down and gave Lucy a quick kiss on the cheek. "You deserve it, after everything you've done."

"You see, Lucy," Lord Grave explained, "I felt it wasn't fair for you to carry on being a servant when all the Hard Times Hall orphans have been given

homes where they live as one of the family. Except for Becky, of course, but that was her choice."

"But I'm not an orphan. I still have a family."

"I know that. But what's happened recently has made me rethink some of my ideas, which I admit can be rather old-fashioned. It's about time you stopped being a servant. I want you as my right-hand woman full time. I should have done this before. I'm very sorry I didn't."

Lucy gazed around the room again. Was it really all hers? And to be Lord Grave's right-hand woman, a full-time member of MAAM, well, she couldn't think of anything better. Although, on the other hand, she'd miss Mrs Crawley and the others.

As if he guessed what she'd been thinking, Lord Grave said gently, "You can still go down to the kitchen to see Mrs Crawley and the rest of them. Any time you wish."

"Luce, I think you'd better let me test out this 'ere mattress for you," Smell said. He jumped up on to Lucy's new bed and began kneading the satin quilt before settling himself down. He closed his eye and

was soon snoring gently. A few moments later, everyone was holding their noses as a vile smell began wafting about the room.

"Oh dear," Lucy said, her eyes watering. "I think Smell must be dreaming a bit too hard!"

THE END

ACKNOWLEDGEMENTS

Huge thanks to . . .

As ever, my awesome agent, Kate Shaw. Harriet Wilson, whose editorial wisdom has taught me so much, and the rest of the team at HarperCollins for their hard work on Goodly and Grave. I'm so proud of what we have created together. The supremely talented Becka Moor, for her always brilliant and witty illustrations.

All my family and friends for their enthusiasm and support, especially Nikki Malcolm, Amanda Harries, Claire Lawton, the Wards, Leo and Vanessa Mantini (we miss you guys!) and The Writing Asylum lunch club, Chris Curran, Tricia Gilbey, Claire Whatley, Jo Reed and Susan Howe.

My husband. I couldn't do any of this without you.

Finally, a special thanks to you, the reader! I hope you've enjoyed Lucy's adventures.

DON'T MISS THE FIRST TWO ADVENTURES!

JUSTINE WINDSOR

GOODLY AND GRAVE

In a Bad Case of Kidnap

Could the mystery of the missing children
be linked to the strange goings-on at Grave Hall?
Lucy is determined to find out . . .

Magical objects are going missing, there's a break-in at Grave Hall and, strangest of all, someone is stealing soil from churchyards. When Lucy digs a little deeper, she starts to suspect these crimes are part of one deadly dangerous plot.

Can she stop a killer in their tracks?